A Thief in Search
of a Baby

B. Heather Mantler

ISBN:1927507359
ISBN-13:9781927507353

Dedicated to everyone from English 126 in the spring
of 2017 for their input in this story.

CHAPTER ONE

If the sounds of the car pulling up outside were not hint enough, the knock on the door let Lydia know the last of the party guests had arrived. She opened the door to the woman and her daughter. The woman was surprised to see Lydia, instead of Caitlyn's mother, Megan.

"Hello, I'm Lydia, Caitlyn's aunt."

"Tiffany Hospkins and my daughter, Grace," the woman said.

"Wonderful," Lydia said, "Come in. The rest of the guests are in the living room."

"Here is the gift," Grace's voice was quiet as she offered the box covered in colourful paper.

"Thank you." Lydia accepted the gift. Grace slipped off her shoes and headed toward the sounds of other girls. Tiffany closed the door before taking off her own shoes.

"Everyone else is in the kitchen," Lydia said.

"Where is Megan?" Tiffany followed Lydia down the hallway. Lydia placed the present on the coffee table with the rest of the gifts and did not answer until she was back in the hallway.

"She found a 'toy' with the same interest in health stuff," Lydia answered, "And apparently there was a retreat, or something, he talked her into going to. She left a note for Dalton about him not being into the same things she was and it being bad to have that kind of negative energy around."

"What about Caitlyn?" Tiffany asked as they entered the kitchen, where three other mothers were seated at the kitchen table.

"The retreat is for adults only," Lydia answered, "But she promises to be back for Caitlyn. Dalton called me to come and help out until the busy season for his job was over."

"Is his job ever not busy?" Jessica Keppler asked.

"Technically, it is three months busy and three months quiet rotation," Lydia answered, "But I think he has been spending more time at work over the last couple years due to avoiding Megan."

"Where is he today?" Tiffany asked as she sat down in the last empty chair.

"Work," Lydia answered, "He tried to get today off, but got called in. Excuse me." Lydia headed down to the freezer. She had left the door at the top of the stairs open and the conversation from the kitchen filtered down to her.

"I wonder what that all means for Megan and Dalton," Tiffany said.

"My husband talked to Dalton yesterday," Jessica said, "According to him, Dalton has filed for divorce from Megan and asked for custody of Caitlyn."

"The court is never going to rule his way," Tiffany said, "Not when his job keeps him so busy."

"Well, Lydia seems to be good for Caitlyn," Jessica said, "She has been here two weeks now and Caitlyn's schedule hasn't been interrupted at all because of it."

"Her job must be pretty flexible for her to help out," Tiffany said.

"I think she works night somewhere," Jessica said, "Because she leaves about nine in the evening. Dalton takes Caitlyn to school and Lydia doesn't appear until she smokes a cigarette on the porch at noon."

"Dalton lets her smoke around Caitlyn?" Tiffany asked.

"Lydia smokes on the front porch and Caitlyn is never there when she does it," Jessica answered, "And as long as she isn't offering one to Caitlyn, I don't think he cares."

"Do you know if Lydia bakes?" Tiffany asked, "Because I had to promise Grace she didn't have to eat a sugarless cake."

"No idea," Jessica answered.

Lydia smiled to herself as she took the ice cream cake out of the freezer and started back up the stairs.

It was just after nine. Lydia relaxed on the porch railing and lit a cigarette. As she exhaled her first drag, the door opened and Dalton stepped outside before closing it behind him. He sat down on the swing.

3

"Caitlyn's asleep," Dalton said.

"She like your gift?" Lydia asked.

"It goes well with the bracelet kit you gave her. Between the kit and that many beads, she's going to be very busy for the next couple weeks."

"At least you wrapped the gift yourself."

"From the sounds of it, you were the perfect birthday mom."

Lydia shrugged.

"Something wrong?"

"I'm not into this domesticity thing." Lydia tapped some ash off her cigarette before taking another drag on it.

"You're good at it. You should try it on a more permanent basis."

"With who? I'm not going to be moving in here and my last lover is dead."

"You shouldn't have too much trouble finding another one."

"That is not the point. I don't want any random guy in my life, or for the possibility of domesticity."

"Well, things at work don't seem to be slowing down and I expected it to do so soon."

"The Houdini Challenge isn't for another month. I'll stay until then."

"Caitlyn likes having you around and I appreciate it."

"It cost you enough."

Dalton let that comment settle as he pushed off and got the swing moving. Lydia stared out at the street for several minutes before turning back to look at Dalton.

"I have to ask," Lydia said, "What is that lingering smell in the upstairs bathroom?"

"Megan burned incense in there," Dalton answered, "I have been trying to air it out since she left."

"You need to fumigate."

"I was hoping time would solve the problem."

"How is that working so far?"

"About as well as anything else involving Megan in my life."

Lydia left that statement hanging in the air as she once again looked out over the street. Dalton did not try to add anything. The creak of the swing became the only sound between them. It lasted several minutes.

"Caitlyn's teacher sent a notice home about career day," Lydia snubbed out her cigarette but did not turn to look at Dalton.

"What happened?" Dalton asked, "She didn't pick from the traditional doctor, lawyer, firefighter."

"No," Lydia said, "The teacher is looking for parents to come in and talk about their professions. Since Caitlyn couldn't tell her teacher what you did for a living, her teacher thinks you would be the perfect person to come in and do a presentation."

"Maybe she would accept Caitlyn's aunt talking about her career."

"Yeah, because going into an elementary class and explaining how to steal secure objects is a good idea. That won't go over well with the teacher or the parents. You just have to go in and explain your work in security. The teacher would be far more accepting."

"And I would have to make up some of what they want to know. Otherwise, I'd have the same problems you have."

"Well, the other option is to send the letter to Megan and suggest being a freak is an interesting career."

"She doesn't consider herself a freak. And she went last year to explain the evils of any diet that wasn't vegan. The teacher was not happy about it and the children spit out the sugarless, wheatless, tasteless cookies. Fortunately, they pitied Caitlyn, not picked on her."

"All the girls today were really happy about the ice cream cake I let Caitlyn pick, but they were worried until I brought the cake out."

"Suppers weren't too bad, but baking and other so-called treats were horrid. I thought it was a fault I could overlook because the rest of our relationship was going alright. Apparently, I was wrong."

"You want commentary from an outside view?"

"No."

"Then I'll just give you my advice. If she tries to come back, continue with the divorce proceedings."

"Your advice is unnecessary. I don't need that freak in my life, nor does Caitlyn; though I'm going to have to convince a judge of that if Megan tries to claim custody. Being a vegan, in and of itself, is not considered child abuse."

"But leaving your daughter to join a much younger man at a meditation retreat without any mention of the girl in the note? That might be the more persuasive argument, especially when you add in that she did so when she was supposed to be picking her daughter up from school."

"But I'm busy most of the time and even at eight, they frown on leaving a child alone. Not to mention that statistically, the courts are more likely to award custody to the mother."

"That is changing these days. I knew a guy who was able to get full custody of his two children, despite their mother fighting for it."

"What was his secret?"

"The daughter testified the mother's boyfriend tried to rape her. When the daughter went to her mother to complain, the mother ignored it and the father listened."

"I don't have anything like that and I don't want anything like it."

Lydia looked at her watch.

"I suppose I'm keeping you from work," Dalton said.

"I know you have stuff to do," Lydia replied.

"Touché," Dalton nodded. He got to his feet and walked to the door. He opened it but turned back before stepping inside.

"Have a good night," Dalton said.

"Of course," Lydia said.

Dalton went inside and closed the door behind him. Lydia dropped off the porch railing onto the lawn and headed for the rental car parked at the curb.

Lydia wasn't worried about getting work, so she ordered a double scotch and sat in a booth near the bathrooms. It was the best spot to watch the entertainment without being accosted. She had already given up her keys and credit card number to the bartender in an effort not to be bothered by anyone, except when she needed another drink.

A woman came into the bar who definitely didn't belong. Her brown hair was pulled back in a loose ponytail, her blue jeans were work jeans, and her shirt reached her wrists as well as her neck. Also her runners matched her jeans. She looked around the bar as if searching for someone specific.

Lydia felt the urge to duck down out of sight but did not give in because she knew the woman was unlikely to see her back in the corner. The woman could also be looking for anyone and not necessary Lydia. The woman went to the bar and tried to get the bartender's attention, which took a few minutes because he was busy filling the orders coming in. Finally, she managed to get him to stop long enough to ask her question. The bartender shook his head and went back to filling orders. She followed him down the bar, going around the people on the stools. She was begging him to provide her with the information she desired.

Lydia knew the woman was looking for her. The woman did not look like the type of person who typically paid for Lydia's services, which meant more work for less pay or the possibility of pro bono work. On the plus side, Lydia didn't need the money for rent or food, but on the other side, the Houdini Challenge was in a month and she didn't want to take a job which would interfere with her plans to compete in that.

The bartender kept shaking his head, but the woman persisted. Finally, the woman managed to convince the bartender of her need, or he decided he wasn't getting paid enough to be harassed, he pointed to the booth where Lydia was sitting. The woman left the bar and approached.

"Lydia Sumerton?" the woman asked once she was standing beside the booth.

"Maybe," Lydia replied, "Why?"

"My name is Elizabeth James," the woman moved her hand as if she was wondering whether she should hold it out to shake, "I need your help."

"I don't offer help," Lydia said, "I am paid for my services."

"Tyler Durand sent me to you," Elizabeth twisted her fingers, "He said you would help me if I offered to pay you for your services. I don't have much, but I will pay you what I can."

Lydia studied Elizabeth for a very long minute as Elizabeth continued to twist her fingers.

"How do you know Tyler Durand?" Lydia asked.

"We went to school together," Elizabeth answered, "We have kept in touch over the years. When I told him my situation, he suggested I come to you."

Lydia studied Elizabeth for another minute before nodding toward the vacant side of the booth. Elizabeth sat down quickly as if she was scared Lydia might change her mind.

"What are you looking for exactly?" Lydia took out her notebook, sipped her drink, and waited for Elizabeth to start. Elizabeth hesitated as she took a deep breath and readied herself.

"My baby has been stolen," Elizabeth said, "And I need to get her back."

"This sounds like a job for the police," Lydia said.

"I filed a report and they have been working on it," Elizabeth said, "But months have gone by without them finding anything. The more time it takes to investigate the case the less time and energy they have to put into it."

"And you think I can help?" Lydia asked, "I am not in law enforcement or any other profession, which would be useful to your situation. There are plenty of agencies around who can help you.

"I have been to many of them," Elizabeth said, "And they try, but really they can't help."

"So, why me?" Lydia asked.

"Tyler said you are a thief," Elizabeth answered, "Which means you can go places and get information unavailable to the public. You can find out what happened to my child."

"I'm an independent contractor with certain moral ambiguity," Lydia said, "But I don't think that will help you much."

"No one else has been able to help me," Elizabeth's voice caught in her throat and she took a deep breath before continuing, "I promise to pay you for your time."

Lydia was quiet and sipped her drink. Elizabeth clasped her upper arms and waited. Occasionally she would let out the breath she was holding. Lydia waved down the server for another drink and did not speak until it arrived.

"Tell me what happened."

"About a year ago I was foolish about things and had a one night stand with a guy I met at a club," Elizabeth said, "I never learned his name and I don't particularly care now. Two months later I found out I was pregnant. It didn't bother me to be a single mother, so I assumed I was out of the dating pool."

Elizabeth paused as she played one handed with the napkin from Lydia's first drink. Her eyes were watching the activity rather than looking up at Lydia.

"Then I met this bastard, who portrayed himself as a gentleman, while I was in the doctor's office. He told me he was there because his sister needed a ride and he couldn't turn her down when she was six months pregnant."

The napkin was ripped from the abuse and Elizabeth tried to leave it alone. However, she was soon back to folding and unfolding it.

"We got along quite well, but I didn't think I would ever see him again. Then a week later he showed up at the coffee shop I frequent. He had some explanation about why he was there, which at the time I believed."

The napkin was starting to look like it was on its way to being confetti. Elizabeth had given up trying to leave it alone and was using both hands to shred it.

"We talked about it and he claimed to be okay dating someone who was pregnant with someone else's baby. At the time I thought it was rare and precious. He occasionally wouldn't be able to meet up some days because his sister needed him. According to him, the father of her baby wasn't around either and he did what he could to support her. As I got closer to my due date, he had more and more time for me. He supported me through my final two months to the point where I gave him a key to my apartment. When I went into labour, he was there at my side. I was in the hospital for three days because the nurses wanted to make sure I knew what I was doing when I took Ella home. He was around for those days and even got me a ride home when I was released. Ella and I had been home a week and he was visiting regularly."

Elizabeth paused again. This time the napkin was in too many pieces to shred further. Elizabeth looked up to find Lydia watching her. The blue eyes were emotionless and gave no sign of the thoughts behind them. Elizabeth turned her own eyes to her hands and she twisted them. With a deep breath, she continued her story.

"One evening Ella was crying and I was sleeping. He was there and said he was going to get Ella for me. I must have gone back to sleep because I don't remember hearing anything. When I woke up both of them were gone. I called the police, but I knew so little about him and where he would go that I was not able to answer their questions."

Lydia waited, but Elizabeth didn't have anything more to say. Elizabeth was breathing in and out deeply like someone trying not to lose control.

"Did anyone else you went to find anything?" Lydia asked.

"The lady at the women's shelter on Grove Way took down the description," Elizabeth said, "Then she said the description matched one of a man who had done something similar to one of their clients. But I couldn't speak with the client because, according to one of the other people who work there, she committed suicide within three months of it happening. Something about the loss of her child and postpartum depression."

"I need the name he gave you and the name he gave her, if you have it," Lydia said.

"He told me his name was Michael Jonson," Elizabeth said, "And his sister was Melanie. The other woman's name is Grace Hardin and the name he gave her was Christopher Holmes."

"Date of your daughter's birth?" Lydia made some notes.

"February eighteenth," Elizabeth answered, "I've spent the last three months trying to get help from various people."

"Had you visited the doctor before meeting this Michael, or was this the first visit?" Lydia asked.

"I met Michael on my third visit to the doctor," Elizabeth answered.

"And the doctor's name?" Lydia asked.

"Dr. Eric Spencer," Elizabeth answered.

"The address of his office?" Lydia asked.

"The office building on Barley," Elizabeth answered, "On the third floor. I haven't been back to him since Ella was born as she was healthy and so was I."

"Did this man, who called himself Michael, give you any personal information that would be helpful?" Lydia asked.

"He worked weekdays, usually until five," Elizabeth paused between statements to think, "Whenever we got a meal together, I was my choice as to what kind of food we ate. I got the feeling he preferred Italian and didn't like Chinese food." "He had money to spend, or at least he never had any problem paying for things. I don't know what kind job he had." "Occasionally he would wear pricier clothing and he seemed more comfortable wearing that than the casual clothing he wore when he came around." "I can't think of anything else. He was such a good listener and didn't say much about himself."

Lydia was quiet as she studied the notes she had written down. Elizabeth looked up from the table at Lydia. Whatever thoughts were going around in Lydia's head they were not visible on her face. Elizabeth rubbed her hands together and occasionally would rub a hand up and down her arm.

"Can you help me?" Elizabeth finally could not stand the quiet anymore.

"I'm not sure a thief is what you should be looking for," Lydia answered, "And I don't work for free."

"I don't have a lot," Elizabeth said, "But I'll pay you what I can. Please, no one I have talked to has been able to help. The police are investigating, but they have other cases they have to work on. I talk to the detective every other day and he assures me he is doing what he can. But it has been three months since I have seen my daughter, Ella."

"Leave your number with me and I will let you know what I come up with," Lydia said, "But don't expect much."

Elizabeth wrote her number down on a napkin before handing it to Lydia.

"Thank you," Elizabeth said. Then she got up and left the bar. Lydia took another sip of her drink. She was going to enjoy this one because it seemed fate had decided she was not going to get drunk tonight.

Lydia was just finishing her drink when the bartender sat down across from her. His replacement was already serving up drinks behind the bar.

"Sorry about directing her to you," the bartender said, "But she wasn't going to leave me alone otherwise."

"Desperation does that to people," Lydia said, "And she is very desperate."

"Another pro bono?" the bartender asked.

"Not quite," Lydia answered, "But I'm not expecting much out of it."

"I'll get you your keys before I head out for my cigarette," the bartender said before getting up. He went behind the bar briefly and avoided taking orders while there. The bartender dropped off Lydia's keys before heading into the back. Lydia took them and put them into her pocket as she got to her feet.

She followed the bartender out the door in the back. The stock room was empty of people and the back door was propped open. Lydia slipped out and into the alley way. She and the bartender nodded to each other as she went by him towards the entrance to the alley.

Lydia skipped going to her car and headed down the street. She walked the three blocks over from the bar to Grove Way. The women's shelter was half-way up the block. Most of the lights were off, but there was one on in the back. She pulled on the handle, but the door was locked. Her first thought was to pick the lock and then thought better of it. Instead, she knocked on the door.

For a few minutes, it appeared as if no one was coming and then movement in the darkened building became visible. As the person got close to the glass, Lydia could see that it was a woman. She was in jeans and a sweater. Her hair was pulled back from her face. The woman carried herself as if she was the director of the organization. She unlocked the door and opened it a small bit.

"Yes?" the woman asked.

"A woman named Elizabeth asked me to find her daughter Ella," Lydia answered, "She said she had come here for help and was told another woman had a problem with the same man. I was wondering if you could give me a few minutes of your time to answer some questions."

"Are you with the police?" the woman asked.

"No," Lydia answered, "I am an independent contractor."

"A private detective?" the woman asked with distaste.

"No," Lydia answered, "Just someone Elizabeth was desperate enough to turn to."

"I remember Elizabeth," the woman said, "But I'm not sure there is much I can tell you."

"I'm not looking for anything confidential," Lydia said, "Just information which could help track down Elizabeth's baby."

The woman studied Lydia as she made the decision about trusting Lydia. Lydia did not try to convince the woman of her sincerity or her trustworthiness. Finally, the woman opened the door to let Lydia in before closing it and locking it behind her.

"I'm Natalie," the woman said as she led the way to the office in the back of the building.

"Lydia," Lydia said.

"McKing's Lydia?" Natalie asked.

"I wouldn't say that," Lydia answered, "But I have worked with him in the past."

"He has helped us out a few times," Natalie said, "He has talked about you and working with you on some of his jobs."

"I only work with him when he agrees to pay me," Lydia said, "Elizabeth agreed to pay me for my help, though I don't expect much."

"You only work when you're paid?" Natalie asked as they entered the office. There was a desk piled with files and paperwork, a desk chair, and a second chair for visitors. Natalie sat down in the desk chair and gestured for Lydia to sit in the other chair, which Lydia did.

"I try to make sure I can pay my bills," Lydia answered, "My standard jobs are a lot different from what Elizabeth asked me to take on."

"I tried to help Elizabeth," Natalie said, "But there was nothing I could really do for her."

"She said her description matched one another woman had given you," Lydia said, "A Grace Hardin."

"Yes, Grace met a man similar to the one Elizabeth talked about," Natalie said, "She was a lot more vulnerable than Grace."

"Elizabeth said she is dead," Elizabeth said.

"Elizabeth was correct on that fact," Natalie said.

"I'm going to guess the reason behind her death is not the same one Elizabeth gave me."

"Grace first showed up at our door running from an abusive relationship. We helped her in whatever way we could. Mostly she needed a hiding place and a fresh start. She found she was pregnant once she was here, but unlike many others she didn't return to her husband for support."

"What about her abuser?"

"He showed up a couple times, but he never saw her and we thought he gave up. He refused to sign the divorce papers she sent him. His name was Jerry Hardin and they lived a couple cities away. The only reason he followed her here was because she put this agency as her address in the paperwork."

"Where did she meet the man who stole her child?"

"I am not sure exactly," Natalie sighed, "I hadn't seen her in a couple months when she came in to introduce me to her new born son. Christopher wasn't with her, but she couldn't find anything negative to say about him. She showed me a picture of the three of them."

"All he had to do was smile at her and not hit her, and she melted into his scheme."

"She had never dated anyone except her husband. No other man had noticed her before or during her marriage. I tried to get as much information about Christopher as I could while she was here because I was very worried he was going to take advantage of her vulnerable state."

"What did you learn?"

"Very little," Natalie shrugged, "She really didn't know much about him. He was good at listening, he took her out for Chinese because he didn't like fast food burgers, and he worked an office job."

"High money, low profile?" Lydia asked, "Or low money, low profile?"

"Low money, low profile," Natalie answered, "If he started throwing money around, she would have been far more suspicious of his intentions. His attention was enough to catch her, but when you don't believe you deserve the attention having a rich guy suddenly spending money you on makes you nervous."

"His relationship with Elizabeth suggested he had money, which leaves the question of whether he actually does or whether is it part he played."

"You think he has money?"

"I think he is gaining more of it with each child he steals. But he may have cultivated the attitude of self-deserving throughout his life. Unfortunately, it gives him a range of character roles he could step into."

"You think Grace wasn't the first time?"

"I think this man operating too smoothly for these two cases to be his first."

"I suppose you meet all sorts of con artists in your line of work."

"I meet all sorts of people in general," Lydia said, "Do you know what doctor Grace went to?"

"I referred her to the doctor we usually send clients to, but he has too many patients and gave her file to another doctor," Natalie answered, "She never mentioned the doctor's name, but I didn't ask because I trust the doctor I sent her and I don't believe he would send her to someone who is not trustworthy."

"I'm just trying to figure out who the man is and what happened to Elizabeth's daughter. Did Grace talk about having any family aside from her husband?"

"Yes, but she couldn't go to them for help. She had tried previously, but they couldn't hide her well enough from him. You think you'll find her son?"

"There is that possibility, though I doubt it."

"Tomorrow I am putting up a sign with the man's face on it so people around here can be wary of him, unless you think it will change your chances of finding Elizabeth's daughter."

"I'm not with the police, there is no need to worry about disrupting my case. I think you should do it because people need the warning. I doubt his scheming has stopped at two."

"What will you do when you find him?"

"Turn him and the evidence into the police. I'm a thief, not a problem solver."

"I'm not sure whether I am glad of that or not. As much as I value life, there are some people the world could do without."

"Grace came to you after Christopher disappeared with her child?"

"She came here the afternoon after they disappeared. She had tried to get in touch with Christopher before coming. She had gone to any place she connected with him, but she couldn't find a trace. I encouraged her to call the police. She was terrified that her husband would find her if she did, but eventually I convinced her filing a police report would help her get her child back."

"They came here and talked to her?"

"Their initial conversation was here. Grace agreed to let the officers go back to her place and look over it for any clues. Unfortunately, they couldn't help her much. They took down a report and investigated, but nothing came of it. I did what I could, but my resources are limited."

"She didn't take it well."

"With Christopher's betrayal she gave up on humanity," Natalie sighed, "Every day away from her child was hard on her mental state. When she was here, I would try to talk to her and offer any help I could. One day she came in, we sat and talked. It was a good conversation and she left with a purpose for her life. She had hope for the first time in since her child had gone missing. Then the next day I got the news she had been found dead."

"You don't think she killed herself?" Lydia asked.

"Not when her husband was seen around that afternoon," Natalie answered, "She had gotten so wrapped up in her search for her child she forgot to be careful about him. Someone saw him follow her when she left here. I gave the report to the police, but they insisted on calling it a suicide."

"Need to find a cop into social justice and doing the right thing. If it were other cities I might know someone I could direct your way, but not here."

"As much as I would like that, I'll deal whichever officer comes out. Hopefully more than one starts to champion our cause."

"Probably a better idea."

"Where are you going next?" Natalie asked.

"Not quite sure," Lydia answered.

"Leave a number where I can reach you," Natalie said, "In case more information comes my way."

Lydia took a card out of her pocket and scribbled a number on the back. She offered it to Natalie.

"It is the number for a bar I frequent. The bartender will pass along the message."

"No cell?" Natalie asked taking the card.

"Too many ways to track them," Lydia answered, "And I'm not into tech enough to know how to turn those features off."

"I thought thieves were going high tech these days," Natalie said.

"There is a difference between having a cellphone and using technology to steal things," Lydia said, "And since the bartender is good at getting me the messages, I prefer this method over others."

Lydia stood up. Natalie got to her feet before leading the way to the front door.

"I wish you luck on your search," Natalie said.

"Get that notice up soon," Lydia said, "Maybe it'll save someone else the heartache."

"I will," Natalie said. She unlocked the front door and let Lydia out. Once the door was closed, Natalie locked it again. Lydia headed back down the block.

Lydia had almost reached her vehicle when a car pulled to the curb. She looked over to see McKing in the driver's seat. Lydia bent down to window level.

"You bothering the neighbours?" McKing asked.

"No more than you are," Lydia answered.

"Well, you are out wandering the streets at night," McKing said, "That is usually a sign you're on a job."

"I'm on a job," Lydia said, "But not what you're thinking. My original choice for tonight was to drink."

"Job find you?" McKing asked with a frown.

"Pestered the bartender till he gave me up," Lydia answered, "The kind of charity work you rope me into, but she promised to pay me what little she could."

"Is the job interesting at least?" McKing asked.

"I'm a thief in search of a baby," Lydia answered, "What are you up to?"

"Casing a couple places," McKing answered, "But nothing serious. Need any help?"

"Know a Christopher Holmes or Michael Jonson?" Lydia asked.

"Nope," McKing answered, "Should I know them?"

"I would hope you don't know him," Lydia answered, "But I thought I would ask. I think my next step is to break into a doctor's office."

"That sounds like fun," McKing said, "Where?"

"Are you butting into my job?" Lydia asked.

"I'm bored," McKing answered, "And I'm sure you could use some free help."

Lydia pulled on the door handle and slid into the passenger seat. She fastened the seat belt.

"Dr. Eric Spencer," Lydia said, "Third floor of an office building on Barley."

"That is easy to get into," McKing said, "You could pick a more secure place to break into."

"There is another doctor, but I didn't get his name," Lydia said, "This is just where I need to start."

"Then let's go," McKing said as he pulled away from the curb.

They didn't talk as McKing drove. He stayed in the downtown area while still driving a ways. Then he turned the car into an unmonitored underground parking lot. There were a few other cars parked in the lot. McKing picked a space close to where the others were grouped so as to look like it belonged. Only one car was parked in a corner and it was an expensive make and model.

Lydia and McKing got out of the car. McKing led the way towards the elevator door in the column in the middle of the parking lot. They stopped at the doors, where McKing took out a card and swiped it. The light went from red to green and then there were the sounds of the elevator moving.

"Got a key card to every building in town?" Lydia asked.

"Nah, just the ones I want to come back into," McKing answered, "There are plenty not worth the bother."

The elevator doors opened and they stepped inside. McKing pressed the button for the third floor. There was no music for the thirty-second ride. The door opened and they stepped into a small area with several office doors off it. Each door had a name etched in the frosted glass.

"Dr. Eric Spencer," McKing said gesturing to the second door on the left.

"Let's go see if he is up for visitors," Lydia said. She took out a key and slipped it into the lock. It clicked and the door opened. Lydia put her key back.

The doctor's office had a waiting room, an area for the receptionist, and three doors open to examining rooms. Behind the receptionist desk was the door to the doctor's office. McKing unlocked the door to the doctor's office before they went inside.

"So what are we looking for?" McKing asked, "Because I don't see a lot of valuable stuff being in here."

"Medical records," Lydia answered as she moved toward the shelves holding them.

"For?" McKing asked.

"Elizabeth James and Grace Hardin and Melanie Jonson," Lydia answered.

"Okay," McKing said as he started at the opposite end of the shelving. They worked without speaking.

McKing got half-way through the shelf and stopped. He took out a file.

"Found something?" Lydia asked.

"Felicia," McKing answered.

"Put it back," Lydia said, "She would not appreciate you invading her privacy."

"Her doctor is the one at the clinic on the other side of town," McKing said, "As far as I know she has never seen Dr. Spencer."

"Put the file back," Lydia said.

"Why?" McKing asked.

"Because if you don't, I'll break your fingers," Lydia answered.

"So, invading other people's privacy is okay, but if you know them there is something wrong with it?" McKing asked as he put the file back and went back to looking.

"Ever pick up women in a doctor's waiting room?" Lydia asked.

"No," McKing's tone suggested the idea was weird in his opinion.

"Then we search for his choices, not yours," Lydia said.

"Well, maybe if she was really good looking and didn't seem infectious," McKing said.

"What does infectious look like?" Lydia asked.

McKing didn't answer.

"You and Felicia fighting again?" Lydia asked.

"Not specifically," McKing answered, "She quit speaking to me two weeks ago and I haven't figured out what the problem is yet."

"You weren't listening when she told you?" Lydia asked, "Or is this one of her attempts to scare you straight?"

"Well, since she was talking about me getting a day job before she quit speaking to me," McKing said, "I think it might have to do with me going straight."

"And what would you do?" Lydia asked.

"She found me a job working in an office somewhere," McKing answered, "I think I tuned out at the word insurance."

"She going to leave if she loses this round?" Lydia asked.

"I don't know," McKing answered, "We have talked it out so many times before I thought she had given up on the matter and then suddenly a couple months ago she is back at it. She should know better by now."

"What happened a couple months ago?" Lydia asked, "A change in friends, a death in the family, someone close to her give birth?"

"I think something might have happened to her friend Jackie," McKing said, "Here is a Melanie Jonson." McKing pulled out the file and offered it to Lydia. She took it and started skimming through it.

"What are you looking for?" McKing asked.

"Information," Lydia answered as she went to the desk and used the pen and paper on the desk to make some notes. McKing went back to looking through the files as Lydia continued her looking.

When Lydia was finished, she tucked the paper into her pocket before handing the file back to McKing. He put it back in the place he had marked for it.

"I found James," McKing said taking another file out and offering it to Lydia. Lydia took the file and started skimming through it. After a quick skim, she handed back to him.

"Nothing in there?" McKing asked.

"Nothing useful to me," Lydia answered.

"So, Hardin," McKing said going back to the files.

"Yup," Lydia said, but she had turned her attention to the doctor's desk. She did a quick look at what was on top before she started riffling through the drawers. Lydia closed the last drawer as McKing pulled out the third file. He offered it before sitting down in the desk chair. Lydia leaned against the desk as she skimmed through the file.

"That is interesting," Lydia said.

"That would be a first since we got here," McKing said.

"The doctor wrote down a conversation he had with Grace," Lydia said, "About adoption."

"Was she for it or against it?" McKing asked.

"Against it," Lydia answered.

"Then why even record that they had the conversation?" McKing asked.

"I don't know," Lydia answered, "That is why I find it interesting."

"Anything else in there?" McKing asked.

"Not that I see," Lydia said as she finished her skim. McKing took the file and put it back in its place on the shelf.

"So, what now?" McKing asked.

"Nothing more I can do tonight," Lydia answered.

"Let's get out of here before we get into trouble," McKing said. They left the doctor's office and locked the doors behind them. The elevator hadn't moved. They got inside and pressed the button to go down.

They didn't encounter anyone on the brief trip back down to the parking level or in the parking lot itself. They got back into McKing's car and he drove out of the parking lot.

"Maybe you can talk to Felicia for me," McKing said.

"Because, obviously, another thief is going to convince her that your life of crime should continue," Lydia said.

"You can tell her about the last time I tried to go straight," McKing said.

"Taking an office job to case a building is not the same as going straight," Lydia said, "As much as it might have felt that boring during the time you were doing it."

"I asked Tabitha to talk to her for me," McKing said, "But she refused, said it was a domestic dispute and she didn't get into the middle of those. I tried talking to Jackie, but she wouldn't to see me. I thought about asking Greg, but I'm tired of him hitting on me. I'm running out of options and Felicia refuses to say anything to me."

"I think I might go with Jackie on this one," Lydia said, "It is a domestic dispute that should be avoided. Also, I don't know Felicia well enough to come across as anything other than a voice box for you."

"Can you try anyway?" McKing asked.

"In exchange for what?" Lydia asked, "That type of situation requires danger pay."

"I'll pay your fee for the Houdini Challenge," McKing said.

"Already paid it," Lydia said.

"Really?" McKing asked, "Where'd you get the money?"

"None of your business," Lydia answered.

"A future favour?" McKing asked.

"No matter the outcome of the conversation?" Lydia asked.

"Sure," McKing said after a two-second pause.

"Her number the same?" Lydia asked.

"She hasn't changed it in a while," McKing answered.

"Drop me at my car," Lydia said, "I think I'm done for the night."

"Okay," McKing said.

They didn't talk anymore as McKing drove. When they reached Lydia's car, he pulled next to the curb in behind it. They said good night and she got out. He waited until she was inside the car before driving away.

CHAPTER TWO

Lydia stepped into the noon sunlight and closed the front door. She took out a cigarette as she moved to sit on the railing of the porch. It was quiet along the street as most people were at work and the children were at school. There was a little old lady who lived a couple houses down, but she had quit watching Lydia's middle of the day cigarette because nothing exciting ever happened during that time.

After lighting it, she leaned her head back against the post as she exhaled. Half-way through a cough forced her to sit up. She swung her legs so they hung down the outside of the railing. She waited until the coughing to let up before taking another drag.

There was a noise and she looked up to see the little old lady was peering out the window. The little old lady shook her head before closing the window again. Lydia turned back to her cigarette. As she finished it, she heard the phone ringing. She went inside and reached it before the machine could pick it up.

"Hello?"

"My boss wants me to stay late," Dalton said.

"How late?" Lydia asked.

"Something about eleven or midnight," Dalton answered.

"Remember when you offered to pay me to show up and babysit," Lydia said, "And I told you that you couldn't pay me to take on the job of putting Caitlyn to bed?"

"What am I supposed to do?" Dalton asked, "Ask the neighbour to come and put her to bed while you sit there?"

"Or you could explain to your boss that you have a kid, who needs her father around if he intends to fight to keep custody of her," Lydia said.

"I've worked hard to get this far," Dalton said, "One incident and I slide backwards."

"So, which is more important to you, your job or your daughter?" Lydia asked.

"This is one night," Dalton said, "One night. Why can't you do this for one night?"

"Because if I do it for one night, you'll have me do it for two," Lydia said, "And then I end up Caitlyn's parent, which means I don't get out of here for the Houdini Challenge. If you are going back on our deal, I'm leaving right now and then you definitely need to call the neighbours."

Dalton sighed but did not say anything for a minute.

"I'm going to be in trouble over this," Dalton said.

"Your daughter needs you," Lydia said, "You can find another job. You have never had trouble finding work before."

"I'm only going to be home long enough to tuck her in," Dalton said.

"I'm going out to have another cigarette," Lydia said, "And I'll pick up Caitlyn when she gets off from school."

"Those cigarettes are going to kill you," Dalton said.

"Then my brother can't ask for any more favours from me," Lydia said, "Neither can anyone else."

"I'll see you this evening," Dalton said before he hung up the phone. Lydia put the cordless back on its base. She went back outside to sit down on the railing. Taking out another cigarette she lit it.

Lydia had just about smoked the cigarette down to the butt when she took out her cellphone. She turned it on and watched it boot up. When it was ready, she went through the contact list until she came to Felicia's number. Once hitting the call button, Lydia held the phone to her ear and waited for it to be picked up.

"Hello?" Felicia's voice came on.

"This is Lydia."

"McKing's friend?" Felicia asked.

"Yes," Lydia answered.

"Let me guess, he wants you to convince me to start talking to him again," Felicia said, "Though why I should listen to you, I don't know."

"Because I know you're pregnant," Lydia said.

"How could you possibly know that?" Felicia asked.

"Because I was asked by a woman to find her missing baby and I needed to go through a doctor's files," Lydia answered, "McKing didn't have anything better to do and joined me. He found your file and I convinced him not to read it."

"And you think I owe you for that?" Felicia asked.

"No," Lydia answered, "I think McKing deserves to know what he is losing."

"You aren't trying to convince me to quit trying to change him?" Felicia asked.

"What good would that do?" Lydia said, "You are firm in your position and he thinks he is firm in his position. Tell him what he is losing and walk away. Right now, neither of you are winning. You're just doing as much damage as you can before you destroy him. You might not like his line of work, but I don't think you really mean to cause his destruction."

"You ever loved someone?" Felicia asked.

"Yes," Lydia answered, "For several years. We fought over me being a thief plenty, but I would have never kept a child from him."

"You speak about him in past tense," Felicia said.

"He died," Lydia said, "And it had nothing to do with my line of work. Or me at all. I wish he were still here and we could still fight. If you don't think McKing will change then leave, but he deserves to know what he is losing."

"Does the doctor have anything to do with the missing baby?" Felicia asked.

"I don't know," Lydia answered, "All I know is three women connected to the same man went to the same doctor. Two babies are missing. I haven't talked to the third woman yet. Has the doctor spoke to you about giving your child up for adoption?"

"No," Felicia answered, "I told him that I have a boyfriend."

"The man connecting the women is not the doctor," Lydia said, "Though they are also connected through him. The doctor's connection could just be coincidence and nothing to do with the missing babies. I haven't been able to get far enough in investigating the situations to know and I don't want to start throwing accusations at people."

"If you find the doctor is connected to the missing babies, I would appreciate if you could let me know," Felicia said.

"Tell McKing about the child," Lydia said.

"I'll think about it," Felicia said.

"I'll think about letting you know about the doctor," Lydia said.

"You won't tell McKing about the child?" Felicia asked.

"Not my business," Lydia answered, "Already butting too far into things that aren't my business. But I will know if you tell McKing about the child." Lydia hit the button to end the call. She turned the cellphone off before putting it into her pocket. She took out the piece of paper that had been tucked in beside it. The folded paper had the address for Melanie Jonson on it. There still some time before Caitlyn needed to be picked up from school.

Lydia dropped down to the lawn. Her hand reached into her pocket but rather than taking out the cigarette she wanted, Lydia took out the keys to the rental car. Better to get on with the investigation.

Lydia parked beside the curb in front of a duplex, which was the address for Melanie Jonson. It was in the middle of several residential streets in an area of a middle-class neighbourhood with spots of lower class buildings. All of the surrounding streets were ones where children could safely play in any yard without worries. This duplex had an older car sitting in the driveway, but there were no toys in the yard to suggest children lived in either side. There was a light on somewhere inside, Lydia was headed to the door.

There was no visible doorbell, so Lydia knocked. Nothing suggested anyone was coming until the door opened. The woman standing there was in her late forties or early fifties, dressed in casual clothing, and wore a wedding ring. Her shoulders were stiff while her eyes held a heavy burden and the lines on her face appeared like they had deepened recently

"Yes?" the woman asked.

"I'm looking for Melanie Jonson," Lydia said.

"And you are?" The mention of the name brought some stress into the woman's voice.

"Lydia. I just want to talk to her for a few minutes."

"Not sure how much talking you are going to get out of her," the woman said, "But I guess you can come in."

The woman held the door open for Lydia and then closed it behind her before leading the way down a hallway to the kitchen. At the table was a girl of about eighteen. She was dressed in sweats and her hair hadn't seen a hair brush recently let alone a shower. Her face was lined with grief.

"A visitor," the woman said. The girl did not even look up. Lydia could see the family resemblance between the woman and the girl.

"My name is Lydia," Lydia said as she sat down in the chair next to the girl, "I was hired by a woman named Elizabeth. She said she met a man at a doctor's office and the man claimed to be your brother, who was supporting you through your pregnancy."

"I don't have a brother," Melanie sniffled but did not look up. The woman sat down in the chair across from Lydia with an interest in what was going on.

"But there was a man who showed interest in your pregnancy?" Lydia asked.

The girl gave no indication she heard the question. Her mother did not make any attempt to talk for her daughter, but instead just waited along with Lydia for her daughter to answer.

"You know, sometimes the best way to deal with the pain is to talk about it," Lydia said, "You look like you need to others to help you with the pain."

Melanie looked up at Lydia with sorrowful eyes.

"I want to help you as well as Elizabeth," Lydia said, "But you have to talk to me."

Melanie went back to her hands. It remained quiet in the kitchen for several minutes.

"He said his name was Steven Hardin," Melanie said in a soft voice as she wrapped her arms around her stomach, "He said he was going to take care of me and my baby. The father was into me until I got pregnant and then I had the plague and was ruining his life. He claimed I could have an abortion or give the baby up for adoption so it wouldn't ruin my life too."

"Where did you meet Steven Hardin?" Lydia asked.

"The doctor's office," Melanie answered, "I think he said something about giving a ride to a friend to explain why he was there, but I wasn't really listening. He was so nice and he cared when no one else seemed to. His apartment was nice and he let me move in without expecting me to sleep in his bed with him. He never touched me without my permission." Melanie stopped as the tears started flowing and covered her face with her hands. Her sobs the other thing coming through.

"We were concerned about an older man taking such an interest in Melanie," Melanie's mother said, "But our words were either ignored or reason to start a fight. Do you know who this man is?"

"Not yet," Lydia said, "Elizabeth said he introduced himself as Michael Jonson. He introduced himself to someone else as Christopher Holmes."

"And he stole their babies?" Melanie's mother asked.

"Both children are missing and he was last seen with them," Lydia answered.

"Are you working with the police?" the mother asked.

"No," Lydia answered, "Elizabeth hired me as an independent contractor. However, anything I find will go to the police once I reach the end of what I can do. Right now, I need anything that will help me identify the man."

"Like what?" the mother asked.

"The address to his apartment," Lydia answered, "His job, any information about his friends or acquaintances. I need information to help me identify him."

"He isn't there anymore," Melanie's voice with thick with crying, "The apartment is empty."

"I still need the address," Lydia said. The mother got up and went to the counter by the phone. She went through a pile of notes until she found the one she wanted. She gave Lydia the piece of paper as she sat back down.

"That is the address," the mother said.

"Thank you," Lydia said before turning to Melanie, "He did have a job?"

"He went out at nine and came back at five," Melanie said as she wiped her nose with her sleeve.

"Did he ever talk about his job?" Lydia asked.

"No," Melanie answered, "I asked if his boss minded him taking me to appointments and he said his boss had no problem with it. He never worried about money. He bought baby stuff for me and he even let me pick it out. He just paid for it just like anything else I needed. He said I didn't need to repay him and he didn't want me to think I needed to repay him with sex."

"He cut you off from us," the mother said.

"No," Melanie shook her head, "He didn't care whether I talked to you or not. You both had been so disappointed when you found out I was pregnant that I didn't think I would get much support if I did talk to you."

"This man helped when the baby arrived," Lydia said.

"He supported me," Melanie said, "He only helped when I asked for it. He let me be the mother to Brandon. Until that day. I was tired. Too tired."

Melanie stopped talking to wipe her eyes with hands and then her nose with her sleeve. After a deep breath, she was ready to continue.

"Usually when Brandon cried, I would be wide awake ready to cuddle him and sooth him, but something was wrong. I couldn't move when he cried and it sounded so far away. Sleep kept pulling at me as much as I tried to get up and go to Brandon. I must have fallen asleep despite, fighting to stay awake. I woke hours later and Brandon was gone so was Steven. The building manager was knocking on the door to demand the rent because it was overdue. I didn't have any money and Steven was gone."

"We went to the police," the mother said, "And they looked into the situation, but they didn't seem to be able to find him. He disappeared with a baby and there doesn't seem to be any trace of him."

"Can you find him?" Melanie asked looking up at Lydia for the first time. Her eyes were red from too many tears and her face showed the clutching of hope.

"I am looking for him," Lydia said, "But I don't know yet whether I can find him. He has done the same thing to two other women and I think he may have moved on to another woman, but that doesn't mean I can find him."

"But if he is found, I could get Brandon back?" Melanie asked.

"I don't know," Lydia answered, "It depends on what he did with the child."

"What he did with Brandon?" Melanie asked. The hope was starting to fade.

"Most likely he sold Brandon to someone looking to adopt," Lydia said, "And that situation is a legal one. I don't know how that works."

"If you give the information to the police then it would seem likely that we can work through the legal stuff to get her child back," the mother said putting her hand on her daughter's shoulder. Melanie let herself be comforted as she curled back in on herself.

Lydia ripped the corner off the notepaper and wrote down a phone number.

"If you think of anything that may be of some help, leave a message for me here," Lydia said sliding the piece over to the mother. The mother nodded as she accepted the paper.

"I'll show you out," the mother said as she got to her feet. Lydia stood up and followed the mother to the door.

Lydia got back into her rental car. She looked at the address for the apartment before checking the time. There was still time before she had to pick up Caitlyn from school and the apartment building was not very far away. Lydia turned the car on and pulled away from the curb.

There was parking in the alley behind the apartment building where guests of the tenants could park. Getting into the building itself was easy. It was not a high-end building but there was still some security in place for the tenants. The manager's office was on the main floor. Lydia knocked on the door. It took thirty seconds for the door to be opened by a man, squat in stature and slightly greasy.

"Who are you?" the man asked.

"I am looking for some information about a former tenant," Lydia said.

"You with the police?" the man asked.

"No," Lydia answered.

"All my files are private," the man said.

"I am looking for this man's work address because I really need to talk to him," Lydia said.

"Don't matter who you are or what your con is," the man said, "I don't give out information unless you're with the police."

"Pity," Lydia said.

"No, it ain't," the man said, "I don't know how you got in here, but you need to leave before I call the police for trespassing."

"I doubt the police are going to do much aside from telling you to not waste their time," Lydia said, "Go ahead and call them if you feel the absolute need to. I can wait."

The man did not move, but the expression in his eyes changed slightly as if he was no longer as certain as he had been. He stared at Lydia for several seconds. She met his eyes and held his gaze until he broke eye contact. He shrank slightly into himself.

"Who the hell are you?" the man demanded.

"I am looking for information on the tenant who disappeared with a baby and didn't pay his last month's rent," Lydia said.

"Chris Holmes," the man said, "He didn't say much for the short time he was living here."

"How long was that exactly?" Lydia asked.

"Six months," the man answered, "He didn't leave any forwarding address."

"What about previous addresses?" Lydia asked.

"Cops said they were fake," the man answered, "All the information Chris wrote down on the forms was. Claimed his job was at that big insurance company, but they had never heard of him. I had made the calls to double check things when he moved in and everything checked out. I don't know what I'm supposed to do about things. I gave the information to the cops and they claim everything was fake. Nothing I can do."

"What did you do with his belongings?" Lydia asked.

"Packed them up and put them in storage," the man answered, "Just like I'm supposed to. If he doesn't claim them by year end, I can sell them off to make the rent he missed and the storage costs back. Pricey stuff in there."

"Pricey?" Lydia asked.

"An upgrade on the usual stuff that gets left behind here," the man answered.

"Interesting," Lydia said.

"You ain't got any claim on that stuff," the man said.

"I don't want any claim on his belongings," Lydia said, "I don't even want to see them."

"There ain't much else to tell you about Chris," the man said, "He wasn't social much aside from brief discussions about the weather. Took the girl in without telling me someone else was living there. All roommates are supposed to be approved before they can move in. Only times I saw him talking to other tenants it was about the weather. Those who saw the girl say he said she was his sister. I seen the girl and she ain't his sister unless by different parents."

"Her parental influences aren't in question," Lydia said, "His are."

"Don't know anything about his," the man said.

"Do you remember the times he was home and when he was not?" Lydia asked.

"He worked office hours," the man answered, "Went out in the evenings a lot when he first moved in, but then he stayed in most days. I quit paying attention after that because I had things I had to deal with."

"He have many visitors?" Lydia asked.

"Never saw any," the man answered, "The cops couldn't find anything useful in the stuff he left behind."

"That was why it got left behind," Lydia said, "The phone number under the same name as he gave you?"

"Bill came in the same name," the man answered, "You're better off asking the police about the rest of it."

"If they had any useful information they would likely already have found him," Lydia said.

"You heard my information," the man said, "I don't got any more."

"I believe you," Lydia said.

"You're still trespassing," the man said.

"You need better security," Lydia said. She turned and left through the same door she had entered.

Lydia pulled into one of the free spaces along the school yard. Some of the parents were standing near the entrance while others were outside the fence and the rest were sitting in their vehicles. Lydia got out and leaned on the passenger side of the car while she waited. It was not long before the kids were released and the playground was quickly filled with children.

Caitlyn came out her door and looked around until she spotted Lydia. She ran the distance before wrapping her arms around her aunt.

"Hey, Cait," Lydia said as she returned the hug, "How was your day?"

"The teacher wanted to know if Dad got the notice about career day," Caitlyn said, "And she wanted him to contact her as soon as he has an answer."

"You'll have to talk to him when he gets home," Lydia said, "I told him about the notice, but he didn't give me any sort of answer."

"Do you think he'd do it?" Caitlyn asked excitement filling her eyes.

"I think you have to ask him," Lydia answered, "And add in how much it would mean to you. In the meantime, I thought we could go for ice cream."

"You and Dad had an argument," Caitlyn's smile faded.

"Minor disagreement," Lydia said, "Nothing that won't blow over in the next twenty-four hours."

"It is about me?" Caitlyn asked.

"Naw, it is a sibling thing," Lydia answered, "Why would we argue about you?"

"Because Mom does," Caitlyn said, "And then they both shout."

"No shouting involved," Lydia said, "As I said, it is a minor disagreement between siblings. Nothing you should be worried about."

"Okay," Caitlyn said.

"Unless you want something other than ice cream," Lydia said as she opened the back door.

"The good ice cream place or the one at the park?" Caitlyn asked as she climbed in and buckled her seatbelt.

"The good one," Lydia answered.

"Then ice cream is fine," Caitlyn said. Lydia closed the door and went around to the driver's side. She got in and started the car. It took a minute before she could pull into traffic as the other parents were making the street crowded, but soon they were on their way. Lydia did not try to make conversation but left it up to Caitlyn.

Caitlyn watched out the window for several minutes before she turned toward the front.

"They are getting divorced, aren't they?" Caitlyn asked.

"Yes, they are," Lydia answered.

"Do you think it will make Dad happier if Mom wasn't around?" Caitlyn asked.

"I don't know," Lydia answered, "It might, but only if he is willing to work at it."

"Do you work at being happy?" Caitlyn asked.

"Plenty," Lydia answered.

"Why?" Caitlyn asked.

"Because I lost someone I loved a while ago and if I let it, the sadness would take over my whole life," Lydia said, "I like spending time with you and I don't want to lose these happy times to that sadness."

"Mom said she was only happy when she was eating right and exercising," Caitlyn said.

"Those are things she did for her to work at being happy," Lydia said, "But she must have been happy spending time with you too."

"I don't think so," Caitlyn said.

"Why?" Lydia asked.

"Because she never liked any of the activities I do," Caitlyn said, "She was happy if I went running with her, but she got bored if we sat and coloured together. I don't like running. I don't like helping her make her disgusting cookies, but she acted like making them was so great. I only helped her because otherwise she wouldn't have time for me. Dad will sit and colour with me in the evenings or he'll sit and read with me. I like it when he has does that because he feels happier at those times. But he doesn't seem happy any other time."

"I think your Dad needs to be reminded of what makes him happy," Lydia said.

"We need to take him with us for ice cream one day," Caitlyn said, "He used to like ice cream before Mom switched buying real ice cream for her brand."

"That is a good idea," Lydia said, "You can invite him along later this week."

"Thursday," Caitlyn said, "He is likely to have the time then. He used to come and pick me up on Thursdays."

"Maybe we can convince him to come with me to pick you up on Thursday," Lydia said.

"We have to make sure he isn't busy with work first," Caitlyn said.

"Of course," Lydia said.

Lydia parked in front of the ice cream shop. They both got out of the car and went inside. They had arrived before most of the other parents with school-aged children, so the line-up was short. Caitlyn looked over all the flavours before she picked cookie dough. Lydia chose mint chocolate chip before paying for both cones. Once they had been given the ice cream, Lydia and Caitlyn sat in a booth.

"So, what did you learn at school today?" Lydia asked.

"We had to practice our letters," Caitlyn answered, "The teacher says we need to learn cursive writing, but we do more with computers and don't write much."

"You should learn how to write in cursive," Lydia said, "But you aren't likely to use it beyond third grade."

"Then why do I have to learn it at all?" Caitlyn asked.

"So, that in twenty years people can still read notes written in cursive ten years ago," Lydia answered. She leaned back as she lowered her ice cream cone.

"Are you alright, Auntie?" Caitlyn asked.

Lydia opened her mouth to reply, but instead she started coughing. She put down her ice cream cone. One hand covered her mouth and the other she put on her chest.

"Auntie Lydia?" Caitlyn asked. Lydia could not answer.

Caitlyn slid out of the booth and went to the cash register. The line-up had become longer since they had ordered, but the girl at the register was between customers.

"What can I do for you?" the girl asked.

"My aunt is coughing and she can't stop," Caitlyn said.

"Maybe she needs some water," the girl said. She filled a paper cup before stepping out from behind the counter to follow Caitlyn.

Lydia was still coughing. The girl offered her the cup, but Lydia could not stop long enough to drink and her face was going red. Caitlyn sat on the edge of the booth and licked her ice cream as if it was a nervous tick rather than to stop it from melting on her hand.

The girl set her mouth in a firm line and headed back to the register. Caitlyn watched with concern as Lydia continued to cough. She had closed her eyes and her whole body was slumped. The coughing did not stop.

"Auntie Lydia," Caitlyn's scared voice had Lydia barely opening her eyes. Lydia shook her head.

The girl from behind the counter came back over.

"My auntie can't stop," Caitlyn said.

"It is okay," the girl said in a tone meant to calm Caitlyn, "I called for some help. They should be here shortly."

"Her lips are turning blue," Caitlyn's tone was getting higher. Other people in the shop started to glance over.

"I know," the girl said, "I also know what to do. It'll be okay."

Lydia collapsed on the seat as she quit coughing. The girl grabbed her to prevent injury and laid her out. Then the girl started CPR to get Lydia breathing again.

Caitlyn stayed back out of the way. Other people in the shop had moved towards the action, but still giving room. There were murmurs from the crowd, but Caitlyn's focus was her aunt.

The girl was getting too tired to continue when there was the sound of a siren approaching. One of the customers, who had been standing by and watching, took over doing CPR to give the girl a rest. The ambulance pulled into the parking lot. The attendants came into the shop and quickly over to the booth. The girl explained what happened as they started working. Caitlyn barely heard any of it as she watched her aunt's face for any sign of life.

The ambulance attendants used equipment when they took over for the man. They hadn't been working long when Lydia started breathing on her own. It was not very strong, but she was breathing. The attendants took Lydia out to the ambulance on a stretcher. Caitlyn followed them out. They hooked Lydia up to an oxygen tank in the back of the ambulance.

"This is your aunt?" one attendant asked Caitlyn.

"Yes," Caitlyn answered, "Lydia."

"Do you know if she has any medical conditions?" the attendant asked.

"No," Caitlyn said with a shake of her head, "She smokes, though."

Lydia coughed a couple times before sitting up. The attendant tried to get her to lie back down, but Lydia shook her head. The attendant said something about going to the hospital and Lydia shook her head at that too. She continued to shake her head as the attendant pressed the issue of going to the hospital to be checked out thoroughly. Finally, the attendant suggested she just sit for a few minutes on the oxygen. Caitlyn climbed up into the back of the ambulance to sit next to Lydia.

"I'm alright," Lydia said smiled down at Caitlyn.

"Are you sure?" Caitlyn asked, "Because you stopped breathing."

"I'm alright now," Lydia said.

"You should go to the hospital and be checked out by a doctor," the attendant said.

"That isn't necessary," Lydia said.

"Maybe you should," Caitlyn said, "Just to be sure. My teacher says doctors are supposed to help us feel better."

"I'll be fine without a doctor," Lydia said.

"Okay," the attendant said, but he did not sound like he meant it, "Just sit for a few more minutes on the oxygen to make sure you are alright."

"You didn't get to finish your ice cream," Caitlyn said.

"That is okay," Lydia said, "I can have some another time."

Once the attendants let Lydia off the oxygen, she and Caitlyn got into the car. Lydia drove them home.

Lydia was sitting on the porch railing, but she had not lit the cigarette in her hand. Instead she stared out down the street. It had been a quiet afternoon with Caitlyn unwilling to let Lydia too far out of her sight. Caitlyn even forgot to be upset with her father for not being home for supper.

The front door opened and Dalton stepped out. He did not look happy as he walked over to Lydia.

"What is this about you collapsing this afternoon?" Dalton asked.

"Not a big deal," Lydia answered.

"An ambulance was called," Dalton said, "Caitlyn said she was scared you were going to die."

"I have someone who wants to talk to me this evening," Lydia said, "Are you sticking around or going back to work?"

"You're supposed to be taking care of Caitlyn," Dalton said, "If you are medically unable to do so I need to know."

"As I have told everyone, I am fine," Lydia said, "Are you coming or going?"

"Unfortunately, I have to go," Dalton said, "But you need to make a doctor's appointment."

"If you are going, go," Lydia said, "Or I will and you can explain to your boss why you couldn't."

Dalton opened his mouth to say something but then decided against it. He stalked away. Lydia put the cigarette back in the pack before going inside. She would wait until Dalton came home before she went to see McKing.

McKing was sitting in his car, which was parked at the curb. There was another man sitting in the passenger seat, who Lydia did not recognize. The window was open so Lydia could hear them as she came up alongside the car. She stopped short of the front passenger window to listen

"How long are we going to sit here?" the man asked.

"Until she shows up," McKing answered.

"We've been here for hours," the man said.

Lydia crouched down beside the car so she could see straight through to McKing.

"I was going to stay in tonight," Lydia said, "But then I remembered she wasn't talking to you and you won't know the result of the conversation."

"So, what did she say?" McKing asked.

"That it was none of my business," Lydia answered, "And I agreed with her."

"And?" McKing asked.

"It was a short conversation," Lydia answered.

"I asked you for a favour," McKing said.

"I did," Lydia said, "But she wasn't interested in being convinced to change her mind."

"Fine," McKing said, "I guess I'll have to accept that response."

"You aren't getting another one," Lydia said.

"This is my friend Justin," McKing said pointing at the man in the passenger seat.

Lydia studied the man in the light from the street lamp. He had a young face with neat brown hair and blue-grey eyes.

"I don't mean to be rude," Lydia said, "But I don't need any more friends right now."

"I understand," Justin said, "And I don't take offence."

"We're headed out for a job," McKing said, "Wanna ride along?"

"Problem job?" Lydia asked.

"Not in that way," McKing answered.

"You think I can't get into enough trouble on my own?" Lydia asked.

"Whichever way you want to take it," McKing said.

"I'm tired enough I shouldn't," Lydia said as she opened the back door. She climbed inside. McKing started the car and then pulled away from the curb.

"What are you avoiding?" McKing asked.

"My brother," Lydia answered, "He's started nagging me about my life. He thinks I should find domesticity because I am good at looking after my niece for him."

"That is almost as bad as Felicia before she stopped talking to me," McKing said.

"He's sitting up waiting for me to get back," Lydia said.

"That sounds more serious than wanting you to settle down," McKing said.

"I accidently scared my niece," Lydia said, "And he wants to discuss it."

"Scared her how?" McKing asked.

"If it was your business I would tell you," Lydia answered, "And it was an accident. What is this job?"

"An information run," McKing answered, "A company that doesn't like electronic records. Instead they have a warehouse of paper records."

"I hope you know where to look," Lydia said.

"It's supposed to be organized in such a way as to make finding things easy," McKing said, "And we have directions. It shouldn't take too long to get in and find what we are looking for."

McKing pulled over to the curb in the industrial part of town. He turned off the car.

"I'll stay here and keep watch from the car," Lydia said.

"Okay," McKing said. Lydia held out her hand between the seats. McKing dropped the car keys into it. Then McKing and Justin got out of the car. Lydia did not bother to watch them go; instead she laid out in the back seat and closed her eyes.

Lydia woke to someone knocking on the window. She sat up and looked out. It was not McKing or Justin, but a man in a police uniform. Lydia opened the door and stuck her legs out so she was sitting up.

"Yes?" Lydia asked.

"No overnight parking," the police officer answered pointing up at a sign.

"My friend said he had something he needed to do in the area," Lydia said waving toward the front of the car, "And since I was tired, I asked if I could wait in the car. He should have been back by now. He must have been distracted by something. He tends to be a workaholic."

"Which building does your friend work in?" the officer asked.

"I don't really know," Lydia answered as she took out her cellphone, "The one time I actually visited the building it was daytime and months ago. I have his number here somewhere." She turned the phone on.

"May I look at the vehicle registration?" the officer asked.

"Sure," Lydia answered. The officer went around to the passenger side. The phone finished turning on. She texted McKing's cell to let him know there was a police officer at the car.

"What is your friend's name?" the officer asked as he came back around with the registration in his hand.

"Neal McKing," Lydia answered.

"And your name?" the officer asked.

"Lydia Sumeton," Lydia answered.

"Do you have any ID on you?" the officer asked. Lydia moved to one side so she could take her driver's licence out of her pocket. She offered it to the officer, who took it and examined it. Lydia's phone dinged. McKing had answered.

"He says he is sorry and that he got distracted," Lydia said, "He'll be back in a minute."

"So you're visiting the city?" the officer asked.

"Yes," Lydia answered, "My brother's wife left him and he needed some help looking after his daughter. Since I'm between jobs at the moment, I figured it wouldn't be a problem to help out."

Movement caused Lydia to look down the street. McKing was coming towards the car.

"Here he comes now," Lydia said. The officer looked up at him.

"I am really sorry about this," McKing said when he reached them, "I know there is no overnight parking here. I was just going to be fifteen minutes, but I got distracted."

"May I see some ID?" the officer asked.

"Of course," McKing said taking out his wallet. He handed over his driver's licence.

"You work?" the officer asked.

"I work in the offices above Taverish's welding," McKing answered, "They lock up the parking lot at night and I don't have the privilege of getting a key."

"Very well," the officer said, "This is your first warning. If I see your vehicle parked here again at night, I will have to issue you a ticket."

"Yes, Officer," McKing said.

The officer handed back the driver's licences and the registration paperwork for the car.

"Have a good night," the officer said before going to his car. He got in. Lydia pulled her legs in and closed the back door. McKing got into the driver's seat. Once he got the keys back from Lydia, he started the car and then pulled away from the curb. McKing turned left at the first corner they came to. The officer had not followed them and they were quickly out of sight. At the next corner, McKing pulled over long enough to pick up Justin up from where he was standing with some folders in his hands.

Justin got into the passenger seat and McKing was quickly moving the car through the next intersection.

"When did you get a cell?" McKing asked.

"What's it to you?" Lydia asked.

"Well, considering your long list of reasons not to have one, it seems strange you suddenly have one," McKing answered.

"It became necessary a while ago," Lydia answered, "And I haven't bothered to ditch it, especially since I came back for family responsibilities."

"It was useful for getting you out of trouble tonight," McKing said.

"Since when is sleeping in a parked car illegal?" Lydia said, "At most, I would have gotten to spend the rest of the night someplace not as comfortable. You would be paying the impound charges on your car. What took you so long?"

"The warehouse wasn't as organized as we had been informed," McKing said, "The information was in the general area we had been directed to, but it was a large warehouse and things were scrambled. But we did get what we needed. Have a good nap?"

"I don't remember it," Lydia said, "But I'm still tired."

"I can drop you off at your car," McKing said.

"I left the rental car at my brother's place," Lydia said.

"What did you do? Walk?" McKing asked.

"I borrowed a car," Lydia answered, "Probably best if I don't go back to pick it up."

"Seriously?" McKing asked.

"I guess you'll never know," Lydia answered.

"Justin is parked outside my place," McKing said, "So, we'll head there. How's your job going?"

"It's stalled," Lydia answered, "I've talked to the players I know, but they haven't given me enough to be useful. My next piece is to look into the doctor to see what he has hidden in his life."

"And if he is clean?" McKing asked.

"I start asking his patients questions," Lydia answered, "Until I track down his next victim."

"You don't think he has moved on?" McKing asked.

"To what point and purpose?" Lydia asked, "He has a nice set-up here and the police aren't taking him seriously."

"What do you mean?" Justin asked.

"This guy is stealing babies after befriending their mothers," Lydia answered, "They have reported the crimes to the police without any results. But they aren't doing anything useful like putting his picture out to warn the public about the menace. The guy is stealing babies, shouldn't public safety be considered?"

"They should be taking that very seriously," Justin said.

"But they aren't because it's the mothers making the reports," Lydia said, "So, single women without support and no one to help them raise a fuss. Easy to forget and easy to ignore."

"So, next is looking into the doctor?" McKing asked.

"Probably start with an internet search," Lydia answered, "And see what comes up from there."

"Maybe you can find more patients so you can get more information," McKing said, "Need to go back through his patient files?"

"No," Lydia answered, "If I talk to his patients, I'll find them another way."

McKing pulled into the driveway of his house.

"The kitchen light is on," McKing said, "Felicia should be in bed by now. Maybe she is having trouble sleeping."

The three of them got out of the car. Justin did not head to his vehicle, which was parked at the curb. Instead, he followed Lydia and McKing to the porch. McKing unlocked the door. They went inside.

"Felicia?" McKing called without being too loud. He walked through to the kitchen. There was no one in the room, just a folded note on the table. It had McKing's name on it. He picked it up and unfolded it.

Lydia tapped Justin on the shoulder and nodded toward the living room. Then Justin followed her as she left the kitchen. The street lamps provided the only light in the room by which they sat down. They did not say anything as they sat there.

It was a good fifteen minutes before McKing came into the living room. He did not bother to turn on the lights. Instead, he just sat down.

"She's gone," McKing's voice was flat, "She says she'll only come back if I quit being a thief and take the job opportunity she lined up for me."

"At least she is giving you a chance," Lydia said.

"I can't do it," McKing said, "My whole life has made me into the thief I am today. You can't just turn that off and pretend it never happened."

"When love is at stake, you have to decide what you can do and what you can't do," Lydia said.

"When you talked to her today, did she say anything about leaving?" McKing asked, "Did she say anything that would suggest where she would go?"

"I don't have the answers you're looking for," Lydia said, "She gave all the answers you're gonna get in her note."

"But she is asking the impossible," McKing said.

"Then you need to decide whether you can do the impossible or whether you are going to give her up," Justin said, "Because I don't think she is going to change her mind unless you change."

"You said insurance company the other day," Lydia said.

"Yes, why?" McKing asked.

"It is nothing," Lydia said, "But when I talked to the manager of the apartment building where the guy lived, he said that on the guy's application he listed his job with an insurance company. Except according to the police who talked to the manager later, they said no one by that name had worked there."

"Maybe he did work at an insurance company," McKing said, "Under a different name. Have you asked around at the companies?"

"I don't have a picture of him," Lydia answered, "And I don't know what name he would be going by because all of them so far have been false. It makes it really hard to ask around about him."

"You know-" McKing started.

"No," Lydia said, "If you start working for the insurance company, you do so to please Felicia, not to help me with my investigation. I will figure out who the guy is without any such help from you."

"You said you were stuck," McKing said, "And that you needed to look into the doctor in hopes of finding him."

"Those are my problems," Lydia said, "If you give Felicia false hope and then claim it was just to help me, I will find someone willing to put you in the hospital."

"You aren't going to do it yourself?" McKing asked, "That is a change."

"I'm not in as good a shape as I should be," Lydia answered, "I get winded just walking upstairs."

"Everyone gets winded going up stairs," McKing said, "I read an article about it the other day. It was all science based and everything."

"I'm sure it was," Lydia said, "Threat still stands."

"Fine," McKing said, "I won't help you out."

"I think you need to spend some time thinking about what you need to help yourself out," Lydia said.

McKing did not have an immediate response, so the group fell silent.

CHAPTER THREE

Lydia could feel the crick in her neck as she blinked back the sleep and let herself realize there was sunlight invading the room she was in. She was sitting in a chair. It was a living room. There was a man stretched out on the couch under the window.

Memories of being at McKing's house and being introduced to his friend Justin came back to Lydia. She wiped the sleep out of her eyes.

"You wheeze when you sleep," Justin said, though he had given no indication he was awake.

"Just proves I'm still alive," Lydia said.

"And that would be in question?" Justin asked.

"Some days I wonder," Lydia answered, "And other days I hope."

"You hope you're alive, or you hope the opposite?" Justin asked.

"McKing went to bed?" Lydia asked.

"Before dawn showed up," Justin answered, "Probably waking up soon. Though I don't know that for certain."

"I don't know what schedule he keeps," Lydia said, "Never cared before this either." Lydia got out of the chair and stood up.

"Going to find him?" Justin asked.

"I have better things to do with my time," Lydia answered, "Don't you?"

"Do you cook?" Justin asked.

"Only when I have to," Lydia answered, "You're better off finding McKing and asking him."

Lydia left the room. When she came back a few minutes later, Justin had not moved. As she was sitting back down, Lydia's phone chimed. She took it out and checked the message.

"Real life calling for you to get back?" Justin asked.

"No," Lydia answered, "Just a friend checking in. I was staying at her place before my brother called."

Justin did not respond and the room was quiet. Lydia kept doing stuff on her phone. There was no noise from anywhere else in the house.

"How did you meet McKing?" Justin asked after a while.

"I was in the city for my brother's wedding," Lydia said, "And I went looking for trouble. McKing wasn't hard to find from there. How did you meet him?"

"We were introduced though a friend because I needed help getting into a building," Justin said, "Not that I couldn't have done it on my own, so much as I needed another person to pull off my plan."

"McKing is good at helping people," Lydia said.

"Most people seem to believe he is a good thief in his own right," Justin said.

"He is not bad there either," Lydia said.

"Not much for heaping praise, are you?" Justin asked.

"He has been caught," Lydia answered, "You wanna be a good thief, you don't get caught."

"You ever been caught?" Justin asked.

"No," Lydia answered, "As far as the police are concerned I am an honest citizen."

"Not even been suspected?" Justin asked.

"There was one cop once upon a time," Lydia answered, "But he could never prove anything and everyone else thought he had gone off his rocker."

"Why did they believe that?" Justin asked.

"Because by that point he was spouting some highly questionable theories about things," Lydia answered, "He was retired before he could get too deep into the case."

There was the sound of someone else moving in the house. The sound of the bathroom door closing and a few minutes later opening. After some shuffling, McKing entered the living room. He slumped down into the same chair as he had been sitting in last night.

"Texting someone?" McKing asked when he noticed Lydia's attention was on her phone.

"Research," Lydia answered, "Figured I would see what came up if I looked up the doctor."

"Found anything?" McKing asked.

"Did you know you can rate doctors?" Lydia asked.

"What like leaving reviews of restaurants?" McKing asked, "I think I have heard of such things. The doctor have good reviews or bad ones?"

"Apparently he is good at medicine," Lydia answered.

"But?" McKing asked.

"Bedside manner could use come improvement," Lydia answered, "But there is nothing truly useful in the reviews. Nor on any of the websites discussing doctors. Apparently he is a clean as his hands after they have been sterilized. Which is a good thing if you are looking for a doctor."

"Why don't you make an appointment with him?" McKing asked, "Maybe you can find out more about him that way. Or you can be in the waiting room when a man starts hitting on a pregnant lady in the next chair."

"Because I can't make an appointment to see him," Lydia said, "I don't have the qualifying medical issue for his specialty."

"What?" McKing asked.

"Me and doctors don't get along," Lydia answered. Justin looked over at Lydia with a raised eyebrow. She ignored him.

"So, what is next in your investigation?" McKing asked.

"Don't know yet," Lydia answered, "I have some thinking to do about it. What is your next step?"

"I don't know," McKing answered, "I have some major decisions ahead of me and I don't think one night of sleep is going to be enough to think them through."

"Probably a good idea," Lydia said, "Any jobs hanging around you need doing?"

"Not set up," McKing said, "I just have to drop off the information we picked up yesterday."

"That makes it easier to move on the other things," Lydia said.

"Don't you need to get back to your brother's house?" McKing asked.

"It is only eleven," Lydia answered, "I don't need to be around to pick up my niece until two thirty."

"And your brother isn't already calling you to find where you are?" McKing asked.

"To what number?" Lydia replied.

"You are holding a cellphone," McKing said.

"Which he doesn't know exists," Lydia said, "Last number I gave him was for the apartment where I was staying before he asked me to come back here."

"Wouldn't it be a good idea to give him the number for your cell in case something happens to your niece?" McKing asked.

"No," Lydia answered, "Then he would abuse the privilege."

"He is your brother," Justin said, "Why do you have so many problems with him?"

"Because I dislike people telling me what I should do with my life," Lydia said, "And since our parents are dead, he feels that it is his job. If anyone could track down Alicia, I'm sure he would do the same to her. But since no one can I get all the crap."

"Who is Alicia?" McKing asked.

"The younger sister," Lydia answered. The cellphone pinged.

"Another text from your friend?" Justin asked.

"No," Lydia answered, "A job offer."

"Gonna take it?" Justin asked.

"Can't," Lydia answered, "Too far away. I can't get there and be back in time."

"The job happening this evening?" McKing asked.

"No," Lydia answered, "Tomorrow, but I still can't get there and back in time. Besides they only offer me a part in their jobs when they are really desperate."

"Does that mean you have to offer them an alternative?" McKing asked.

"No," Lydia answered, "That means I text them to say I can't do it and they have to find an alternative. If you want work you have to find your own sources. Besides you don't want to travel that far either."

"I don't know, getting out of town sounds like it might be a good idea," McKing said.

"Running from your problems isn't going to help you," Lydia said.

"I wasn't thinking any permanent moves," McKing said.

"Is there breakfast around here?" Justin asked.

"I don't know," McKing answered, "I don't cook."

"Danny's serves an all-day breakfast," Lydia said, "They also serve a variety of lunch dishes too."

Lydia's cellphone pinged again. She checked it before putting the cellphone into her pocket.

"It is down the block, right?" Justin asked as he sat up.

"Yes," Lydia answered as she moved to the edge of her chair.

"I think I'll sit this one out," McKing said.

Lydia got to her feet as did Justin. They left McKing sitting there as they left the house. Rather than take Justin's car, they walked the couple blocks to the Danny's restaurant. It was open, but not busy. They were seated quickly and a waitress took their order as soon as they had closed the menus.

"So, why aren't you looking for anymore friends?" Justin asked as he sat back in the booth.

"Because I lost someone," Lydia answered, "And any new friends feel like I'm trying to replace him with them."

"He must have been close to you," Justin said.

"We were lovers for several years," Lydia said, "And that is something I don't take lightly. He wasn't a thief. He had a steady job, house, and his biggest secret was that I didn't hold the job he told people I did."

"Sometimes that works out," Justin said, "And sometimes it leads to fights like McKing and his girlfriend."

"We fought about it," Lydia said, "But never to the point of McKing and Felicia. He understood I was a thief before we met and I wasn't likely to change my career path because we were together. The main times we argued about it was when one of my jobs interfered with some event that was meaningful to him."

"What did you tell Felicia?" Justin asked.

"That she should have a talk with McKing before she took off," Lydia answered, "That he deserved to hear what she had to say before there wasn't a chance. You got a girlfriend?"

"Not in a while," Justin said.

"Ever had a fight over your career?" Lydia asked.

"Once or twice," Justin answered.

"A relationship ending fight?" Lydia asked.

"Once," Justin answered, "But we hadn't been together long enough for it to be a big argument or for it to last beyond that fight. What did your friend die of?

"Hypoxemia," Lydia answered.

"Low blood oxygen," Justin said.

"Most people want to know what that means," Lydia said

"My father died of lung cancer," Justin said, "That was one of those terms the doctors threw around carelessly like it should mean something, so I looked it up."

"He survive it?" Lydia asked.

"No," Justin answered, "It was found too late because his doctor thought he had pneumonia and that it would clear up with some drugs along with warmer weather. By the time they realized it was something more serious it wasn't just in the lungs."

"I'm sorry," Lydia said.

"He was doomed from a young age," Justin said, "He never smoked a day in his life, but his parents smoked several packs a day between them and he lived in the smog they created. My grandmother was still alive at his funeral. After watching her son buried, she lit a cigarette as she was being taken away by the car. She died two months later from pneumonia. Her smoking was a contributing factor."

"I'm guessing you don't smoke," Lydia said.

"I don't even stick around when someone else lights up," Justin said.

"I'll keep that in mind," Lydia said.

"Watching your friend choke to death hasn't convinced you to kick the habit?" Justin asked.

"It did until the cravings got too much," Lydia answered, "It was too much all at once. I tend to smoke more when I am stressed, otherwise I smoke about two cigarettes a day to keep the cravings at bay."

"It is killing you," Justin said.

"So I've been told," Lydia said, "Every time I go to a doctor they suggest I quit to extend my life."

"And you see no reason to listen?" Justin asked.

Lydia shrugged. Before any more could be said the waitress brought their food.

After they had eaten, each paid their own bill and they left. Justin headed back to McKing's house to get his car. Lydia called a cab to get her back to her brother's house.

Lydia found Dalton's car in the driveway when the cab dropped her off. She stopped on the porch and lit a cigarette rather than go inside. Apparently Dalton had been watching for her because he came out as she settled against the railing. He sat down on the swing.

"Caitlyn was almost panicky that you hadn't gotten home last night," Dalton said, "I told her you would be fine and probably just got caught up in visiting with your friends."

"I fell asleep when I should have been coming back," Lydia said, "Nothing to worry about. Did you agree to Thursday?"

"Yes," Dalton said, "I got the time off from work."

"Your boss doesn't mind?" Lydia asked.

"Business is starting to slow down," Dalton answered, "I might slide on the list of people to call in for jobs, but otherwise everything else will be the same."

"You need this time with Caitlyn," Lydia said, "I'm not going to be around to help out forever. I have the Houdini Challenge and my own life."

"I had plenty of time to think about it last night," Dalton said.

"And?" Lydia sked.

"I have discussed my hours with my boss," Dalton answered, "And I can get the time I need to take care of Caitlyn while still working enough hours to pay for everything. When things get busy again, there might be a few days when I need to find someone to look after her. But otherwise I have it covered."

"Good," Lydia said, "Then I don't have to stick around."

"I paid for you to be around until the Houdini Challenge," Dalton said, "Unless you plan on paying me back some of that money."

"Fine," Lydia said.

"Caitlyn said you had a coughing fit so bad you passed out and needed oxygen," Dalton said.

"And she would be observant," Lydia said.

"What is going on?" Dalton asked.

"That is between me and my doctor," Lydia answered.

"You don't have a doctor," Dalton said.

"Still doesn't make it any of your business," Lydia said, "I am sorry it happened when I was with Caitlyn and I hope it doesn't happen again."

"You should probably pick up Caitlyn," Dalton said, "Because if I show up, she'll assume we are headed to the morgue to identify your body."

"You need to teach your kid not to worry so much," Lydia said, "I'm not that close to death."

"I'll work on it," Dalton said. He stood up and went into the house.

Caitlyn was glad to see her aunt at two-thirty and even happier when her father was able to join them for ice cream on Thursday. Both Caitlyn and Lydia were happy to hear that Dalton had agreed to visit the class for career day. Dalton spent a lot more time at the house and with his daughter.

Friday Lydia waited until after the usual time for her cigarette before leaving the house and heading down to the bar. McKing was sitting at her table. Lydia thought about finding someplace else to sit but decided she might as well sit with McKing. She sat down across from him. He had a glass of beer in front of him and appeared to have indulged in a few before her arrival.

"How goes the thinking?" Lydia asked after she had ordered a drink from the passing server.

"I already finished my thinking," McKing answered, "I started at the insurance company yesterday."

"But?" Lydia asked.

"Felicia isn't coming back," McKing answered, "She says it is too early for her to come back."

"Makes sense," Lydia said, "She wants to know you are serious and two days isn't enough for her to see that. You have to survive at least a week at the job."

"You have any jobs set up for this weekend?" McKing asked.

"Nope," Lydia answered, "Haven't been looking either."

"What about your investigation?" McKing asked.

"At a standstill for the moment," Lydia answered, "But that is fine since I've had some ideas as to where to get more information there. None of which I need help with."

"You're just avoiding giving me openings where I would slip up," McKing said.

"A valid and true point," Lydia said, "If you are going to change for Felicia, you have to actually change and not just appear to change."

"I'm trying," McKing said, "But it is so boring. What do these people do for entertainment?"

"Look around," Lydia said, "What are people doing?"

McKing looked around at the other people in the bar. The server brought Lydia her drink.

"They are getting drunk," McKing said.

"And that right there is the answer to your question," Lydia said, "Though I hear some people have hobbies."

"What am I supposed to do?" McKing asked, "Take up knitting?"

"Metalworking, woodworking, garage tinkering," Lydia answered, "Plenty of options to choose from."

"Do you have a hobby?" McKing asked.

"Telling people to piss off," Lydia answered, "After they give me advice about my life."

"I'm not sure that counts as a hobby," McKing said.

"Well, since I spend so much time doing it, I figure it must count as one," Lydia said, "And if people left me alone about it all, I could find better uses of my time."

"Have you tried adoption agencies?" McKing asked.

"I have looked up the ones in the city," Lydia answered, "But I haven't gone into their places of business to check on them physically."

"Anything had about them on the internet?" McKing asked.

"The better business bureau has one marked as having questionable business ethics," Lydia answered, "But they don't state the hows and whys of that statement. I was going to check them out first."

"Need some help?" McKing asked.

"Nope," Lydia answered, "And I won't from you unless Felicia tells me it is okay."

"I was thinking Justin may need some work," McKing said.

"This is a non-paying job," Lydia said, "I'm not sure I want to bring someone in and waste their time when they could find paying jobs."

"I can't say whether he would have problems with that or not," McKing said, "But if you need help he may be available."

"I'll think about it," Lydia said, "But only if I find I need help. However, most people who are willing to help without a steady cheque or some other way to get paid isn't someone I want to work with."

"They aren't all undercover cops," McKing said.

"Enough are for me to want to avoid such situations," Lydia said, "That is part why I don't get caught."

"I haven't been caught in many years," McKing said, "But I have been working to make sure I'm not caught since then."

"What do you know about Justin?" Lydia asked.

"He's been around a couple years," McKing answered, "We met because he needed a second person for a job. It wasn't a hard job, just needed two people. He definitely isn't in your league."

"He attach himself to you or does he find his own jobs?" Lydia asked.

"I call him when I need him," McKing answered, "Otherwise I don't hear much from him. I hear about his jobs occasionally, but most of them are minor in the overall picture. He has never been caught that I know about. Might have a lot to do with them being small jobs, or he doesn't do much above his level. I doubt he is undercover."

"But you don't know for sure," Lydia said.

"If you are working on tracking down missing babies, having an undercover cop might be beneficial," McKing said.

"There might be some truth there," Lydia said, "But I still don't like working with cops. I don't mind giving them the information after I found it. I just don't like working with cops."

"I can look further into his background," McKing said, "If you are going need his help. If you don't, I won't look."

"Give me a chance to look into the adoption agency first," Lydia said, "And then I'll know more about what I need help with."

"Makes sense," McKing said.

"But don't do anything that will cause you further issues with Felicia," Lydia said.

"I won't," McKing replied.

The server came by and set down new drinks for both of them. She placed a card in front of Lydia before moving on. Lydia put her hand over the card before McKing could read it.

"Work?" McKing asked.

"Don't know yet," Lydia answered, "I am not expecting any message." She slid the card off the table and glanced down at it.

"Really important?" McKing asked, "Or just interesting?"

Lydia did not immediately answer as she studied the card McKing left her to her contemplating while he took a drink of his beer.

"What do you know about Natalie?" Lydia asked finally looking up at him.

"Natalie?" McKing asked.

"She works at the women's shelter on Grove," Lydia answered.

"I help her out occasionally," McKing said, "But I mostly know her through Felicia, who volunteers down there. Natalie cares a lot about her cause and will do whatever it takes to help out any woman who shows up at the shelter's door. Some people might refer to her as obsessed or overzealous, but she had a good heart. Why?"

"Apparently she knows you aren't supposed to be working," Lydia said.

"Does she know you don't work pro bono?" McKing asked, "Because if she doesn't, you better tell her before you get anywhere near the job she needs doing. I can call Justin and see if he would be willing."

"She knows," Lydia said, "And I'll talk to her before handing the job off on to someone else. Excuse me."

Lydia got up and went around the bar to the store room area. She sat down at the desk. All the employees were out front. Lydia dialed the number on the card. It barely rang once before it was picked up.

"Hello?" Natalie's voice came through.

"I just got your message," Lydia said.

"That was quicker than I thought it might be," Natalie said, "But that is a good thing because this is an emergency and McKing is out of service. Yes, I remember what you said about being paid and I have some funds I can pay you from. Though it isn't much."

"You want me to come there?" Lydia asked, "Or explain it over the phone?"

"It would be best if you could come here," Natalie answered, "Unless that doesn't work for you."

"I have all night," Lydia said, "I just need a few minutes to pay my bill and get there."

"Knock on the door when you arrive," Natalie said.

"See you soon," Lydia said. She put the phone back. Lydia went back out to the bar and sat down on her chair.

"Big job or little job?" McKing asked.

"Don't know yet," Lydia answered, "Just scheduled an appointment. Need to pay my tab and head out."

"I'll get your tab," McKing said.

"Are you sure?" Lydia asked.

"Yeah," McKing answered.

"Thanks," Lydia said. She got up and made her way to the exit.

Lydia headed down the street and walked the distance to the women's shelter. Lydia knocked on the door. Almost instantly she could see Natalie's profile in the darkness of the building. Natalie became more visible when she reached the door. Once the door was unlocked, Natalie held it open for Lydia to enter. Natalie locked it before leading the way to her office.

"Thank you for coming," Natalie said as they sat down.

"What do you need?" Lydia asked.

"I need you to break into a place and steal a person," Natalie answered, "This woman had come in and needed help getting away from her husband, but she couldn't just leave at that moment for some reason. She thought she could get away again. However, she phoned today to say she was trapped in the house by her husband."

"I know you put trust in these people and what they tell you," Lydia said, "But I need to cover my ass. Are you sure this is on the up and up?"

"I have checked out what she had told me," Natalie said, "And everything checked out. I understand about you wanting to make sure it isn't a trap."

"If you feel it is okay then I'll trust you," Lydia said.

"Thank you," Natalie said, "I thought it might be best if I drive. Then I am there, so she knows everything it okay. But I will only be able to do that after you bring her out. Legally I can't step inside the house."

"That should be fine," Lydia said, "Does she know to expect someone?"

"I said I would get someone there as soon as possible," Natalie said, "So, as long as you identify yourself as being there because of me it should be fine."

"Okay," Lydia said, "I think I am ready."

"Good," Natalie said. She started gathering her things together to get ready herself. Once she was ready, Lydia stood up and they left the office. Lydia followed Natalie through the hallway to the back door. When they had gone through to the parking lot, the door locked behind them.

Natalie's car was the only one in the small lot. They got into the car. Natalie had put her briefcase in the trunk before getting into the driver's seat. She started the car. When she was ready, Natalie pulled out of the parking lot and into the late night traffic.

Lydia kept watching the scenery they passed. Natalie focused on driving.

"So, you heard about Felicia and McKing's fight," Lydia said.

"She said she had given him an ultimatum," Natalie said, "She said that if possible I shouldn't ask for his help with anything illegal."

"That was pretty much what she left on the note for him," Lydia said, "She said she would only come back if he got the job at the insurance company and gave up being a thief."

"How is he doing with it?" Natalie asked.

"He is down at the bar getting drunk to take the edge off his boredom," Lydia answered.

"That isn't going to keep him out of trouble," Natalie said.

"It will for tonight," Lydia said, "There is still hope in him that she'll come back, so he'll drink himself into a depression tonight. Another time and place it might be different."

"But she might not go back to him," Natalie said.

"He isn't thinking about that right now," Lydia said, "Which is the best place for him now. Without that hope, he'll sink into a real depression and be useless for a while. Then he'll go back to being a thief, but he'll start taking jobs he shouldn't and put himself in danger."

"You think she'll take him back," Natalie said.

"I don't know her well enough to know that," Lydia said, "But I got the feeling she is more likely to if he makes an attempt."

"I suppose that is possible," Natalie said.

"You probably know her better than I do," Lydia said, "But one of those things she hasn't told him is what will send her back."

"She is keeping secrets from him?" Natalie asked. She stared at Lydia long enough that she just about swerved into the curb, but caught herself in time to avoid an accident.

"I learned it by accident," Lydia said, "And when he asked me to talk to her because he hoped I could convince her to not try and change him, I suggested she should tell him, but she didn't."

"She shouldn't be keeping secrets from him," Natalie said.

"It is her choice," Lydia said, "As much as I might disagree with it."

Natalie did not respond as she had drifted into deep thought. She did keep the car on the road and headed to their destination. Lydia noticed they were into the upper-scale neighbourhood, where the houses had gates hiding the long driveways and the houses were not necessarily visible from the road.

"We are coming up on the place," Natalie said as she turned right onto a street similar to the last one, "I don't want to stop in front of the house, or even slow down too much."

"As long as you point it out as we go by," Lydia said, "I can figure things out from there. Park on the next street over."

"Okay," Natalie said.

About the middle of the street, Natalie pointed to a house fairly close to the curb. The fence around it was metal bars with a security gate and cameras at regular intervals. The house was large with a main building and wings on either side. There didn't appear to be any guards wandering the grounds or dogs.

Then they were passed. Natalie had kept the same speed all the way along the street so as not to appear suspicious. Then she did as Lydia said and parked on the next street over. There was a park with a playground. Natalie parked next to the curb farthest from the street lamp.

"I don't know anything about the house," Natalie said, "Or where she is in the house. Her name is Bethany."

"I'll figure it out," Lydia said as she pressed the button to unbuckle the seat belt, "If I am not back in an hour, you should probably get out of here."

"Are you sure?" Natalie asked.

"If it is over an hour, I've been caught and you should get out of here," Lydia answered.

"Okay," Natalie said, "Good luck."

Lydia got out of the car. She headed down the street back towards where the house was.

When she reached the house, Lydia walked passed. She checked for where in the house the lights were on. Reaching the other side of the property, Lydia was careful to stay out of sight of the cameras as she went over the fence. There were plenty of shrubs and other such to hide behind on the way to the door.

The camera above the door scanned the area in front of the steps, but not directly in front of the door. Lydia waited for the camera to reach the other side of the step before moving to the door. She tried to knob and it opened. After a quick glance inside, Lydia stepped in and closed the door behind her. There was no click of it locking, so Lydia felt safer.

There was a small entry way that opened up to a much larger entry way with a grand staircase to the second floor. There were doors on either side of the room and there appeared to be some more on the other side of the staircase. No one people were visible and Lydia could not see any security cameras.

Lydia moved into the larger area. She went up the staircase. Her footsteps echoed slightly on the marble, despite her attempts to be quiet. At the top, Lydia went to the left. In this direction was a large hallway with doors on both sides at regular intervals. They were all closed, but Lydia did not bother with them because she could not see light coming around them.

It was fairly far down the hallway when Lydia saw light coming from one of the rooms. She got close and put her ear close to the door. There were two people inside talking. Both of them were unhappy, but their exact words were hard to make out. It was a man and a woman arguing. Lydia got closer to the bottom of the door where most of the light was coming from.

"Like he is going to believe you," the man voice was saying, "There is no mark on you to prove I touched you."

"He doesn't need proof," the female said, "He'll believe me because of what I say."

"I talked to him earlier today," the male voice sneered, "We had a long talk about your mental state. He agrees with me about what should be done with you."

"He would never agree to such a thing," the female screamed.

"Don't worry," the male voice said, "He'll be kept up to date on your progress."

Lydia realized the male voice was coming towards the door. She scurried back to the previous door and pushed it open. Slipping inside, Lydia put her back to the wall and closed the door until it was only open a crack. The room she was hiding in was a bedroom, but it didn't appear to be in use at the moment.

The male exited the other room and closed the door behind him. It also sounded like he locked it. Then his footfalls went by in the hallway. Whoever it was, he was unconcerned about anything in the hallway. Once the footfalls died away, Lydia pushed the door open enough to look out. No one was in sight.

Lydia left the room and closed the door again. She moved to the next door, where the light was coming from. Taking out her penlight, Lydia examined the lock. It was not one of those easily picked, but it was not one that would keep her out for very long. With another check around for trouble, Lydia slipped out her tool case. She selected the tool she wanted and got to work. Several minutes went by before there was the click of the lock. Lydia put her tools away. Then she tried the knob. The door opened.

This was a bedroom similar to the last one, but this one was lived in. There was clothing and other personal possessions scattered around. Not to mention the woman standing at the window with her arms crossed over her chest. The woman turned when there was none of the usual sounds of the male.

"If you are looking for valuables you should try the office on the first floor," the woman said.

"Are you Bethany?" Lydia asked.

"Yes," the woman answered.

"Natalie sent me to get you," Lydia said.

"I thought she would send someone who would knock on the front door," Bethany said as she suddenly started moving. She grabbed her jacket and her purse before exiting the room.

"She didn't seem to feel such actions would be of much use," Lydia said as they started down the hallway.

"They wouldn't," Bethany said, "But I was going to use the distraction to get out."

"Let's see if we can get out without the distraction," Lydia said. Bethany did not say any more as they went.

They did not meet anyone before getting to the staircase. Lydia stopped them there as she checked over the railing. There was still no sign of anyone.

"No servants?" Lydia asked.

"They go home for the night," Bethany answered.

"Security?" Lydia asked.

"Four," Bethany answered, "But I don't know where they are stationed."

"Wait here," Lydia said. Bethany nodded.

Lydia moved quietly as she could on her way down the stairs. Her shoes still made noise on the marble. Lydia checked the area over as she listened for the presence of anyone else. She could not hear or see anyone, but her gut was sending messages about someone being there.

She reached the bottom of the stairs without anyone coming out. Lydia went around the back of the staircase, but did not see anyone in the darkened area. She tried one of the doors. It opened into appeared to be a back hallway. There was a light on further inside. Lydia propped the door open before going further inside. Around a wall, Lydia found an open kitchen. The four security guys were sitting at a counter eating and talking. They had not heard or seen her.

Lydia slipped back and closed the door behind her. It did not have a lock. She took out some glue and applied it to the where the door and frame met. Lydia checked the other door and found it went areas for servants. She glued this door as well. Lydia used the glue on the other two doors on either side of the entry area.

When she was finished, Lydia went to the smaller area in front of the door. There were no obstacles to leaving she could see. Lydia tapped lightly on the wall. Bethany looked over the railing. Lydia signalled for her to come down. Bethany quickly came down the stairs while trying to be as quiet as possible.

"This seems too easy," Bethany whispered when she had reached Lydia.

"I am aware," Lydia whispered back, "But this may be our only chance. Come on. Once we are outside, get ready to run across the lawn, but don't run for the gate. Go to the right corner of the fence. We'll go over it."

"Okay," Bethany said.

Lydia went to the door. She gently tried the knob. It was still unlocked, but something clicked as the door opened. Suddenly a loud alarm went off. Lydia and Bethany scrambled outside. Bethany headed straight to the corner. Lydia closed the door before following her.

They could hear activity behind them. Once they reached the fence, Lydia helped Bethany over before climbing it herself. Instead of running down the street, Lydia grabbed Bethany and pulled her down into the bushes of the neighbour's yard. They both stayed still.

A moment later the door burst open and all four security men came out. They spread out and started looking over the grounds. There were not many places to hide, so they quickly gathered at the front gate. They opened it only enough for three of them to go though, while the fourth stood guard. The three went in separate directions.

One came around the side of the fence where Lydia and Bethany were hiding. He walked between the fence and the bushes. In the dark, he missed seeing them. He walked to the end of the fence and came back. Again he did not see them as he went by. He joined the others at the front gate, where they appeared to discuss what they should do next.

"We have to get out of here," Bethany whispered.

"We will," Lydia whispered back, "But if we run now, we'll be caught."

The two of the security headed back into the house, while the other two stayed at the gate.

"They are reporting to Raymond," Bethany whispered, "And likely getting a car."

"Any way to get to the next street by going through the properties?" Lydia asked, "Because that is where Natalie is waiting with the car."

"All the properties have security," Bethany said, "But there is a sort of path on the other side of this house."

"Come on then," Lydia said. She wiggled under the bush and into the neighbour's yard, which was hidden from the street by the hedges and bushes. Lydia stayed near the ground as she checked over the yard. Bethany came through and dusted herself off without standing up.

"Keep close to the hedge," Lydia said before starting along the route she had pointed to Bethany. She stayed in the crouched position while staying out of the light from the house. Bethany followed her.

They reached the other side of the property and went under the bushes. Lydia kept them hidden by the bush as she looked around. There were no vehicle visible in the street, nor were there any people around. Between the houses were a few feet of space that ran through to the other street.

Lydia stayed close to the hedge as she stood up. She moved along being careful of any security that might get in the way. Bethany followed. They got most of the way through before Lydia froze with Bethany barely stopping before bumping into her.

"What's wrong?" Bethany whispered.

"Trip wire." Lydia pointed down to something at her feet. Bethany started to bend to get a closer look, but Lydia pressed her back into the hedge as headlights went passed on the street. The vehicle was moving slow, but did not adjust its speed.

"Keep your back to the hedge," Lydia said, "And step exactly where I step."

Bethany nodded and focused on Lydia's feet. Lydia was careful as she lifted her feet. She moved forward like someone checking for landmines. Bethany only put her feet only where Lydia had firmly placed hers. They moved like that over several feet before Lydia was less careful with her feet. The vehicle had not come back.

"We're safe," Lydia said. They moved normally through the rest of the path. Reaching the other end, Lydia stopped and checked the street. Natalie was still in her car near the park. There was no one else around. Bethany started to move forward, but Lydia stopped her.

"What is it?" Bethany asked.

"My gut," Lydia answered, "Get down." Bethany crouched down. Lydia lay down in the grass on her stomach. Headlines came visible from somewhere down the street. Bethany dropped to her stomach. They stayed there as the car went by at a steady but slow speed. It continued passed them. Lydia signalled for Bethany to stay down. They waited until they could no longer hear the vehicle. Then Lydia moved forward to check the street.

After a moment, Lydia gestured to Bethany to get up. They both got to their feet. Being watchful, Lydia crossed the street with Bethany behind her. When they reached the other side, Natalie had seen them and started the car. Arriving at the car, Lydia got into the back leaving Bethany to get into the passenger seat. Natalie barely gave them time to get their seatbelts on before she was pulling away from the curb.

"Thank you," Bethany said to Natalie.

"Let's get you somewhere safe," Natalie said.

They did not say anything more as Natalie drove. Lydia slumped down in the backseat until all she could see out the window was the dark sky and the street lamps. She let her mind go blank and fell into a trance like state where she was only conscious of the lights and sky and nothing else.

Lydia barely registered that the car had stopped and two car doors closing. The light stayed still. Time must have past. The car door opened and then closed.

"You asleep?" Natalie's voice came from a distance.

"No," Lydia responded, "Just letting my mind rest. She settled in?"

"As much as she can be at the moment," Natalie answered, "Is it fine to drop you off back downtown?"

"My car is parked a couple blocks from the shelter," Lydia said.

"What is your usual rate for a job like tonight?" Natalie asked.

"A few hundred," Lydia answered.

"Only a few hundred?" Natalie asked.

"For a simple find and retrieve, yes," Lydia answered, "Anything more and I'd be accused of inflating my rates."

There was some shuffling from the front seat, but Lydia's eyes were still staring up passed the street lamp into the night sky.

"Here," Natalie offered an envelope when the shuffling stopped. Lydia took it and tucked it away. Natalie started the car and it was moving again. Lydia let herself come back to the present. She blinked a couple times and brought her eyes back into focus. Then she sat up.

"Back now?" Natalie asked.

"Mostly," Lydia answered, "There are still some effects take longer to disappear."

"You almost looked like you were dead when I got back in the car," Natalie said.

"Still alive and breathing so far," Lydia said.

"Have you gotten anywhere with your search for Elizabeth's child?" Natalie asked.

"Not really," Lydia answered, "I found another victim. Did you get a picture to put up on the bulletin board?"

"Yes," Natalie answered, "I had a poster made up so people could take one if they wanted a copy."

"I'll have to come in for a copy at some point," Lydia said, "Do you know anything about the Kids and co adoption agency?"

"I've heard suggestions that they don't worry about ethics or moral policies," Natalie said, "But not much else. The shelter doesn't deal with them. We have a different agency we refer our clients to. One we know how they work and have fully checked out."

"Makes sense," Lydia said, "Especially if the other one has questionable business practices."

"You think they might be connected to this guy stealing babies?" Natalie asked.

"I don't know yet," Lydia answered, "I was just trying to think of what he would do with the babies once he stole them. He isn't likely to keep them and if he is sticking around for the next victim he isn't going very far to pass them off."

"One would think he would have to go farther before having the babies adopted out," Natalie said, "The police would surely check out the adoption agencies if a baby is missing."

"They may not be adopted locally," Lydia said, "Kids and co have several offices across the country. He drops off the babies, they get taken to another city to be adopted. He doesn't have to go far and isn't likely to get caught."

"So, you need to find evidence against both him and the adoption agency for Elizabeth to get her child back," Natalie said.

"I expected as much," Lydia said, "Plus the added in factor of the adoptive parents, who may or may not believe they adopted legally and don't want to give up the baby they have been caring for over the last several months."

"That part is pretty bad," Natalie said, "Because they have become caretakers to someone else's baby thinking the child is theirs."

"It seems like a hard thing to go through," Lydia said.

"You don't have kids?" Natalie asked.

"No," Lydia answered, "I just have my niece. I've never felt I was in a place in my life where having children makes sense and none of my relationships have been the kind that developed into having children."

"Children tend to develop on their own whether the relationship is ready or not," Natalie said.

"I've worked hard to keep them from developing," Lydia replied, "And right now there are no worries."

"Not in a relationship?" Natalie asked.

"Not ready for any new relationships," Lydia answered.

"Last one didn't end well?" Natalie asked.

"He died," Lydia answered.

"That is a bad end to a relationship," Natalie said. She pulled her car over to the curb. Before turning to

Lydia, Natalie went through her purse. She pulled out a paper and offered it to Lydia.

"A copy of the poster you wanted," Natalie said.

"Thank you," Lydia said.

"I appreciate you help," Natalie said, "Even if I did have to pay for it."

"You know how to contact me," Lydia said before opening the car door. She got out and closed the door. Natalie waved before pulling away from the curb. Lydia watched her drive off before checking where she was. Natalie had dropped Lydia between the shelter and the bar. It was a short walk back to the rental car.

CHAPTER FOUR

Lydia took a drag from her cigarette as she watched a yellow Kia Soul pull up to the curb in front of the house. Megan Sumerton got out of the passenger side and an orange haired muscle man got out of the driver's side. Megan's brown hair was braided back out of her face, but it was already coming loose. She was wearing her skin tight yoga pants and matching workout 'top'. The guy was in track pants and tight t-shirt. He was also checking Lydia out as they came up the front walk.

"What do you think you are doing?" Megan stopped just short of the porch and stared at the cigarette in Lydia's hand, "You are smoking at a house where a child lives."

"What do you think you're doing?" Lydia asked, "Bringing your boytoy to the house of your separated husband and child. Your child is not out here on the porch, but in the backyard playing catch with her father."

"You shouldn't smoke anywhere near a child," Megan started up the steps.

"And you should talk to Dalton before you try entering his house," Lydia said.

"This is my house," Megan said, "I don't need permission to get some things."

"The lawyer hasn't spoken with you, I guess," Lydia said, "I would suggest you talk to Dalton or his attorney."

Megan took another step up the stairs.

"Around back," Lydia pointed toward the gate.

"This is my-" Megan started.

"Around back," Lydia's tone was calm but firm.

Megan stood there for thirty seconds before going back down the steps and heading for the backyard.

"Hey," the muscle man's tone was suggestive.

"You can shove it up your ass," Lydia responded in a cold tone. The muscle man backed off and went back to the car to wait for Megan.

Less than five minutes later the shouting started. More a female voice than male. Lydia was sure her name was mentioned at least once and Caitlyn multiple times. There was one final scream and then the slamming of the back gate. Megan came around the house in a huff. She stalked straight to the vehicle without even a glance in Lydia's direction. Both her and the boytoy got into the car and drove off. Lydia lit another cigarette as she watched them go.

Lydia was sitting on the porch railing when Dalton came out and sat down on the swing.

"Caitlyn in bed?" Lydia asked.

"But not asleep," Dalton answered, "She is scared her mother is going to show up and take her away. I explained to her that her mother can't just take her away and her living situation will be decided in court in a few days."

"You have a court date?" Lydia asked.

"Yeah, the lawyer called yesterday," Dalton answered, "You aren't expected to be there as far as I know."

"Megan might disagree with that," Lydia said, "Or at least want to talk about me."

"I got the feeling she wasn't happy with your presence," Dalton said.

"I was smoking when she showed up," Lydia said.

"You have become the devil incarnate," Dalton said, "That explains some of her blustering."

"From the freak, I'll accept that role," Lydia said.

"You would," Dalton said, "Waiting until you can go to work?"

"Waiting to hear the results of the freak's visit," Lydia said, "Because I didn't think you wanted to talk about it in front of Caitlyn."

"I don't think she needs to hear it," Dalton said, "She is eight and this is adults fighting. Not that I don't talk to her about it, but on her level and her questions."

"So, Megan wants custody," Lydia said.

"She expected Caitlyn to be packed and waiting for her," Dalton said, "Caitlyn told Megan she didn't want to go. Megan then proceeded to chew me out until Caitlyn asked her to leave. At which point Megan finished her name calling before leaving."

"Good for Caitlyn," Lydia said, "She better be in court to give her say."

"The lawyer has been arguing against it," Dalton said, "But I keep telling him she deserves to have her say as to where she lives, especially since Megan and the boytoy don't have a permanent place to live."

"She came here demanding Caitlyn without having a place to live?" Lydia asked, "And she was expecting you to hand the girl over? What is she taking that is rotting her brain so badly?"

Lydia started coughing. Dalton looked at her with concern. It took a minute for Lydia to get the coughing fit under control.

"Need an ambulance?" Dalton asked.

"No, I'm good," Lydia answered still breathless.

"Are you sure?" Dalton asked.

"Yup," Lydia answered, "Just a minor fit; nothing serious."

"You have had more than one serious fit?" Dalton asked, "You need to see a doctor about it."

"I did see a doctor about it," Lydia said, "The first time I had a serious attack."

"And how many have you had?" Dalton asked.

"Four or five," Lydia answered.

"Is there anything you can do to prevent them?" Dalton asked.

"He had some suggestions," Lydia answered, "But I haven't found any particular reason to implement them."

"What about Caitlyn?" Dalton asked, "You scared her the other day and she really doesn't want to lose her aunt."

"She has another one," Lydia said.

"One she doesn't know, who isn't around, and unlikely to meet," Dalton said.

"She doesn't contact you at Christmas?" Lydia asked, "Weird, but I suppose I understand that."

"That sounds like an insult," Dalton said.

"Take it how you will," Lydia said.

"Don't you have to get to work?" Dalton asked.

"As long as you are going inside, so your daughter knows where you are," Lydia said.

"I'm gonna go in and talk to her if she is still awake," Dalton said, "What about you?"

"I got what I wanted," Lydia answered as she stood up, "I might be late coming in."

"You usually are," Dalton said.

Lydia headed down the porch steps. She went along the path to the street where her car was parked.

Lydia had parked her rental car in the parking lot of a restaurant that stayed open late so no one would notice a random vehicle parked on the street. Then she walked the block and a half to the adoption agency. She went around to the back door of the building, which was in the back alley. Before getting close, Lydia pulled her hood down and her face mask up.

When she reached the door, Lydia used her tools to open it. She slipped inside. This was a back hallway with the employee washroom, the break room, a couple offices, and a file room. Lydia tried the file room door and found it required a chip from an ID card. This lock took slightly longer than the back door, but Lydia got through it.

The metal filing cabinets were not locked. The files were also in arranged by month and year. Lydia started three months back and looked through the files. There were several girls who had been adopted out by the agency and none of those shared their name with Elizabeth. However, there was a girl given up for adoption by a man with the last name of Jonson, which was the last name the man had given Elizabeth.

Lydia set that file aside and then moved on to the approximate time Grace Hardin lost her child. It took much longer to find because Lydia did not have a more definite month. But she finally found a file under the name Holmes. The name the man had given to Grace. Lydia set that file with the first one. Lydia went back into the files to see what she could find anything on Melanie's son.

But she could not find any files within the time frame with name Steven Hardin, or any other names Lydia had heard the man going by. There was nothing in the files to suggest any of the boys were Melanie's child. Lydia took the files she had set aside and propped the door open before going down the hallway. The front area had a waiting area with space for children to play than a secretary's desk before several offices. Behind the secretary's desk were several pieces of office equipment. Lydia went to the copy machine.

Lydia copied the entire contents of both files. Then she tucked the copies away in a pocket in the back of her coat. Lydia took the files back to the file room. She returned them to where she had found them. After a quick check to make everything was as she had found it, Lydia left the file room and let the door close.

Lydia went to the back door. She checked the alley way before stepping out. A test of the knob assured Lydia the door was locked. After taking the facemask down, Lydia headed back to her rental car.

When she reached it, Lydia took the papers out and tucked them under the car seat with everything else she had gathered so far. Lydia started the car and headed back to Dalton's house.

Reaching the street, Lydia noticed a yellow Kia Soul parked down the street from the house. She did not see anyone inside it as she drove by. Lydia parked in her usual spot. She went immediately to the house. It appeared normal.

The door was locked causing Lydia to use her key. She locked it once she was inside. Then she stood there and listened. There was a creak from the living room and a groan from the upstairs hallway, but nothing out of the ordinary.

Lydia moved quietly through the front hallway to the kitchen. She checked the kitchen door and found it locked. Lydia went back to the front door and back outside. She did not bother to lock it. Lydia headed down the street to the parked Soul.

When she reached it, Lydia looked in the windows and saw the boytoy curled up in the driver's seat. He looked uncomfortable and was asleep. Lydia knocked on the window. The boytoy jumped and then blinked as he looked around. He uncurled before opening the door.

"Where's Megan?" Lydia asked.

"I don't know," the boytoy answered, "She walked out of a dinner we were having with my friends and I haven't been able to find her since. I thought she might come back here, but I fell asleep waiting for her."

"I think you'll find her somewhere else," Lydia said, "Dalton isn't taking her back."

"I don't even understand why she left," the boytoy said, "We had just finished ordering our drinks."

"Beer?" Lydia asked.

"Yeah," the boytoy answered, "Why?"

"Go home," Lydia said before turning around and heading back to the house.

"Why?" the boytoy called after her.

Lydia ignored him and kept going. He did not call out again, instead she heard the door shut before the engine was turned on. As Lydia reached the walk, there was the sound of the vehicle driving away. Lydia shook her head and went inside for the night.

It was early Monday morning when Raymond Stewart looked up at the sound of knocking at his office door. The chief of security for his office stood there with a file in his hand.

"What is it?" Mr. Stewart waved the man in.

"There was a break-in at the adoption office yesterday night," the chief of security answered.

"That is why I hired you," Mr. Stewart said, "To take care of that kind of thing."

"I am trying, Mr. Stewart," the chief of security said, "But the person was only caught on camera with no other signs she was here and although it looks like she didn't take anything, we don't know if she got what she was looking for."

"Have you taken the picture to the police?" Mr. Stewart asked.

"She is either new to the game, or so good she has never been caught," the chief of security answered, "However, I did speak with a source who identified her as a contestant in the Houdini Challenge, but didn't have any other information on her."

"What is the Houdini Challenge?" Mr. Stewart focused his full attention on the man standing before his desk with a picture out. The picture showed a person dressed in black with a hood blocking most the face. It was almost impossible to tell if the person was male or female.

"Thieves from all over the country gather in one place where they sign up," the chief of security answered, "They are taken to a different city, dropped off on a street corner with only an envelope and no other equipment. In the envelope is the item they are supposed to steal and take back to the place they signed up. They have a week to do this before they are disqualified."

"Which means they have to be pretty good," Mr. Stewart said.

"Those that get in the top ten slots are the best there is," the chief of security said, "But many that aren't so good sign up and fail. There is no level of ability needed to sign up."

"So, is she one of the good ones, or one of the mediocre ones?" Mr. Stewart asked.

"It was suggested that she usually ranks in the top ten," the chief of security answered, "But many years she doesn't finish the challenge."

"And we don't know what she was looking for?" Mr. Stewart asked.

"No, we do not," the chief of security answered.

"Give all the information you have to Kyle Stevenson and let him take it from there," Mr. Stewart said.

"Yes, sir," the chief of security left the office.

Lydia found a space between two other vehicles with occupants waiting to pick up a child from the school. She parked the car and turned the engine off before getting out. She went to stand on the sidewalk to wait. There were some children already on the playground, but a teacher was watching to make sure they did not leave the school grounds before the right time. It was not Caitlyn's class. Parents of those children had drifted to the fence to hold their discussions.

"Lydia, right?" a woman stopped near Lydia.

"That is right," Lydia said.

"I'm Grace's mom, Tiffany," the woman said.

"Right," Lydia said.

"Grace said Caitlyn may not finish the school year at this school," Tiffany said.

"Megan came back on Saturday," Lydia said, "And expected Caitlyn to go with her. However, Dalton has filed for custody and that will not be decided until the court date later this week."

"So, Caitlyn may end up with Megan," Tiffany said.

"It is a possibility," Lydia replied, "But Dalton is fighting for her to stay with him and Caitlyn has expressed her dislike of going with her mother."

"What about Dalton's job?" Tiffany asked, "He is always so busy with his work."

"He has arranged things with his boss, so he is available to be home when she is," Lydia said, "Also I think he will be spending more time at home because Megan will not be there. His work has slowed down for the next three months, which helps."

"Caitlyn must be happy to see her father so much," Tiffany said.

"She would be if she wasn't so worried her mother was going to take her away," Lydia said, "Until Megan showed up, Caitlyn was happier than I had seen her in my time here."

"How long are you going to be around?" Tiffany asked.

"Another three weeks," Lydia answered, "Then I need to get back."

"Your boss must be fairly generous to give you a month off," Tiffany said.

"I do contract work," Lydia said, "So, I don't have a specific schedule and my boss changes with each job. I do have one set up for next month, which is why I have to get back for then."

The bell announced the end of the school day. The students on the playground grabbed their bags and lined up in front of the teacher, who gave them their last instructions for the day before letting them be claimed by their parents.

"Well, it is good for both Caitlyn and Dalton to have you around to help out," Tiffany said, "Until you arrived I didn't know Dalton had any family."

"Our parents died several years ago," Lydia said, "And the rest of us don't tend to visit each other a lot. If he hadn't called asking for my help, I probably only see Caitlyn about twice this year."

"Not very close family," Tiffany said.

"We all lead busy lives," Lydia shrugged.

Students came pouring out of the school to greet parents or climb up the empty playground equipment. Caitlyn and Grace came running towards Lydia and Tiffany. Grace stopped at her mother, but Caitlyn hugged Lydia.

"Can we go for ice cream?" Caitlyn asked. Tiffany raised her eyebrow in a silent question.

"Sure," Lydia answered.

"Ice cream?" Grace turned to her mother with a gleam in her eye.

"You can come along with us, if you want," Lydia said. Caitlyn turned to look at them and nodded.

"I guess we can go get ice cream," Tiffany said, "The ice cream shop near the park?"

"Yes," Lydia said.

"We'll meet you there," Tiffany said. She directed Grace toward their car as Lydia opened the back door of her car for Caitlyn. Once Caitlyn was inside, Lydia closed it and went around to the driver's side. She got in and started the car.

"How was school today?" Lydia asked.

"Fine," Caitlyn answered.

"I forgot to ask about last Thursday," Lydia said, "How did your father's presentation go?"

"He did a good job," Caitlyn said, "He told them he worked in security."

"That is what he does," Lydia said.

"Not quite as he talked about it," Caitlyn said, "Especially during the question part. Why didn't he just tell the truth about his job?"

"Because if he told the whole truth about his work, it would cause the type of security breaches he has been hired to avoid," Lydia answered.

"How are a class of second graders going to be a problem for security?" Caitlyn asked.

"One never knows," Lydia answered, "That is why he needs to be careful. He could also get fired for revealing too much."

"What is your job?" Caitlyn asked, "I asked Dad, but he said to ask you."

"I am currently helping a person find something they lost," Lydia answered.

"Is that what you do all the time?" Caitlyn asked.

"Sometimes," Lydia answered, "Sometimes I take jobs doing other things." Lydia pulled into the parking lot of the ice cream shop and parked. Tiffany and Grace were not there yet. Lydia shut off the engine and turned to look at Caitlyn.

"You aren't going to tell me, are you?" Caitlyn asked.

"I'm a thief," Lydia answered, "People buy me to steal things."

"But stealing is bad," Caitlyn said.

"Yes, it is," Lydia said, "And I don't want you to think otherwise or start doing it."

"But you do it," Caitlyn said.

"As paid employment, yes," Lydia said, "But you should not."

"Why?" Caitlyn asked.

"Because I am an adult and you are a child," Lydia said, "And life isn't fair."

"That's what Dad always tells me," Caitlyn said.

"We learned it from the same source," Lydia replied.

Tiffany pulled into the parking spot beside them.

"I'm not supposed to tell anyone, right?" Caitlyn asked.

"Right," Lydia answered.

"Let's go get ice cream," Caitlyn said as she unbuckled her seatbelt.

They got out as Tiffany and Grace did the same. The four of them went into the ice cream shop. Everyone picked out their flavour and got the cones before Lydia paid for all of them. They took them outside and ate the treat as they walked to the playground at the park.

When Caitlyn and Grace were finished, they went to play on the jungle gym. Lydia and Tiffany sat on a bench. Tiffany did most of the talking with Lydia paying enough attention to respond when required. After an hour or so, Tiffany called Grace and they said good-bye. Lydia noticed Caitlyn come sit but did not say anything.

"Can I ask you a question?" Caitlyn asked. Lydia turned her attention to Caitlyn.

"Sure," Lydia answered.

"If Mom takes me, will you steal me back?" Caitlyn asked.

"There is a lot more to a custody battle than that," Lydia said.

"So, Dad keeps saying," Caitlyn said, "But everyone keeps saying that in custody battles the mothers always gets the child."

"That isn't always true," Lydia said, "But there is a tendency with the courts to sympathize with mothers. However, your father has a strong case. He is also hoping the judge will take your opinion into consideration."

"But what if all that doesn't work?" Caitlyn asked, "What if she gets custody anyway? I can pay you to steal me. I've got twenty dollars saved up from my birthday and Christmas. I was saving it to buy a DS, but this is more important."

"Keep saving your money," Lydia said, "Until the judge makes his decision, there is nothing for you to worry about."

"But what if the judge decides Mom is right?" Caitlyn asked.

"Until there is a decision, there isn't anything to discuss," Lydia replied, "Once the judge has made his decision, we will talk about it. Okay?"

"Okay," Caitlyn's response was subdued. Lydia reached over and put her arm around Caitlyn's shoulders.

"Don't worry about it," Lydia said, "We may not always be around, but family sticks together. Now, come, we should find some proper supper after that ice cream."

"Dad isn't gonna be home for supper?" Caitlyn asked as they stood up.

"Yeah, he phoned earlier," Lydia said.

Caitlyn sighed. They walked toward the parking lot.

Lydia was sitting on the railing smoking a cigarette when Dalton parked his car in the driveway and walked to the porch.

"Caitlyn in bed?" Dalton asked as he stopped on the porch.

"Nope," Lydia answered, "I left her watching TV."

"She has school tomorrow," Dalton said.

"I told you it was your job to put her to bed," Lydia said, "I told you when you asked me to come, I told you last week, and I told you when you phoned today to say you were coming home late. I am not going to change my position. You also need to reassure her that you are fighting for her."

"Why?" Dalton asked.

"Because she wants me to steal her back if her mother gets custody," Lydia answered.

"Shit." Dalton headed inside.

Lydia finished her cigarette before going inside herself.

CHAPTER FIVE

The next evening, Lydia did not stop to smoke her cigarette on the porch at nine because she figured Dalton would come out and want to talk with her. Instead she skipped her cigarette and headed for the bar. Lydia found McKing sitting at her table, but she sat down across from him anyway. The server stopped at the table to deliver a beer to McKing and took Lydia's drink order.

"Still fighting boredom?" Lydia asked once the server was gone.

"Yes," McKing answered, "But that isn't why I am here."

"Then why are you here?" Lydia asked.

"I got an offer on a job," McKing answered, "But I'm not sure you want to take it even if you are interested."

"Why?" Lydia asked.

"Because Kyle Stevenson is asking around about you," McKing answered.

"The name sounds familiar but I can't place it," Lydia said.

"When someone gets Kyle Stevenson's attention they usually end up dead," McKing said.

"Oh, him," Lydia said, "Who would be interested in sending him after me?"

"Not sure," McKing answered, "Anyone in particular you pissed off recently?"

"I checked out the adoption agency on Sunday," Lydia said, "But I'm pretty sure I wasn't recognized."

"Since Kyle Stevenson doesn't have a name, or even a full face as far as I can tell, it is possible the job at the agency is what tipped things," McKing said.

"So, I need to figure out who runs the agency," Lydia said.

"You're going to poke the hornets' nest?" McKing said.

"Never been scared of Kyle Stevenson before, why should I start now?" Lydia asked.

"Have you had him after you before?" McKing asked.

"No," Lydia answered, "But we have a long talk about someone else."

"You've met him?" McKing asked.

"What? You haven't?" Lydia replied.

"You know me, I'm a small time thief," McKing said, "You're the big leagues."

"Not quite that grandiose," Lydia said, "Lots of folks wouldn't count me as an expert thief. I don't go high tech enough or bother with expensive items or really difficult challenges."

The server brought Lydia's drink.

"Do you at least find something at the adoption agency?" McKing asked.

"A couple of files," Lydia answered, "Kids adopted out at the right time period. They are with loving parents half-way across the country now. He used whichever fake name he gave the woman whose baby he stole. Either that or some father with similar names is a big coincidence."

"They let the father put the baby up for adoption?" McKing asked, "I thought the mother had to do that."

"I have never bothered to look into the matter," Lydia answered, "Nor have I ever had a child to give up. I'm not likely to ever have either."

"You're still young," McKing said, "There is still a possibility for you to have children."

"Not up for discussion today," Lydia said, "What is this job you were talking about?"

"A simple break and enter," McKing said, "But I can't do it because I'm still trying to get Felicia back."

"And how is that going?" Lydia asked.

"We are talking every other day or so," McKing answered, "Which is better than before. She still won't come back. Says she isn't sure about me going straight will stick. But we're talking, so I consider it an improvement."

"Good," Lydia said.

"Sometimes I wonder which side of the argument you're on," McKing said.

"I'm not," Lydia said, "I got dragged in kicking and screaming. Remember the whole conversation where you were trying to convince me to phone Felicia and talk to her in return for a future unnamed favour? I didn't want to do it and you wanted to pay my fee for the Houdini Challenge."

"It didn't work," McKing said.

"The favour was owed either way," Lydia said.

"I know," McKing said.

The server brought another beer for McKing and another drink for Lydia.

"You ever get around to checking out Justin?" Lydia asked.

"Still waiting to hear back from a few people," McKing answered.

"So, what is the job?" Lydia asked.

"There is a building slightly outside of town," McKing answered, "There are a few items the client wishes to obtain from the place."

"This sounds like a bigger job than just one person and a toolkit," Lydia said.

"It isn't a tonight job," McKing said, "I haven't talked to Justin about it, because I haven't heard back from people. There are a couple others who could help, but they have their own jobs and lives."

"When?" Lydia asked.

"Friday," McKing answered, "Because people work Monday to Friday, which means the weekend before anyone noticed anything missing."

"No workaholics who do overtime?" Lydia asked.

"Company policy," McKing answered, "Any overtime happens at home because the office has specific hours."

"Got any information on the building?" Lydia asked, "Like schematics."

"Working on it," McKing answered, "But I have to wait until tomorrow to get anything."

"I have to think about it a while longer," Lydia said, "Preferably after you have more information."

"Makes sense," McKing said, "Though if you turn it down, it will leave me scrambling to find someone to take it."

"But you'd find someone," Lydia said.

"Can't leave the client hanging," McKing said, "Even if I can't make any money from the job."

"How's the insurance business?" Lydia asked.

"There isn't enough beer in this bar," McKing answered, "But I am trying. My supervisor thinks I have everything it takes to succeed in the business. I wanted to tell him a trained monkey could do it, but I remembered I needed the job before my mouth opened too far."

"Good idea to keep those thoughts to yourself," Lydia said.

"When I feel the worst, I remember Felicia is worth it," McKing said, "Sometimes I wonder if she is worth it, but then I go back to what I know as a fact. She is worth it."

"Of course, she is worth it," Lydia said, "And if she is talking to you, you are further along than you would be if she hadn't left at all."

"I hadn't thought of that," McKing said, "Another thought to get me through those horrible hours."

"You're welcome," Lydia said. She finished her drink and waved down the server. The server came over and Lydia offered her the money for the drinks with extra for a tip.

"Not going to stay and drink?" McKing asked.

"My brother has his day in court tomorrow over the custody of his daughter," Lydia answered, "And I would like to be awake to talk to him after it is over. Being hungover won't help the discussion any."

"The court usually awards custody to the mother," McKing said, "So, you might be the one to console him."

"I think he has a pretty good case," Lydia said, "At least for this round. She doesn't have any place to live and thus no place for her daughter. He owns the house they live in and has gotten his boss to change his schedule so he isn't working when she is off. He is fighting sympathy with facts."

"Well, good luck to him," McKing said.

"Good night," Lydia said. She got up and left the bar.

Lydia was sitting on the porch railing when Dalton's car pulled into the driveway. She had put out her cigarette before she had even seen his car, so it was not in evidence when Caitlyn and Dalton came down the path. Caitlyn was skipping as she went.

"Good news then?" Lydia asked when they reached the porch.

"Go in and get your school bag," Dalton told Caitlyn before she could respond to Lydia.

"Okay," Caitlyn sounded disappointed, but did as she was told.

"The judge granted custody to me," Dalton said, "Based on my more stable living situation, but Megan can come visit practically anytime and she can take me back to court after she gets a more permanent living situation. The judge assumed Caitlyn would be better with Megan and the lawyer refused to let Caitlyn have a say in where she wanted to live."

"She back with the boytoy?" Lydia asked.

"I don't know," Dalton answered, "I didn't see him. What was the issue between them?"

"He didn't have a clue," Lydia said, "But he also told me she had walked out of a dinner with friends after he ordered a beer."

Dalton started to say something but was interrupted by Caitlyn coming out with her backpack. She ran over to Lydia for a hug.

"I get to stay with Dad," Caitlyn announced.

"Great," Lydia said with a smile, "See you didn't have to worry after all."

"Come, Cait," Dalton said, "We need to get you to school. I promised your teacher that I would get you back to school before lunch was over."

"Okay," Caitlyn said.

"I'll see you after school," Lydia said.

"See you," Caitlyn said before following Dalton back to his car.

Lydia watched them leave. Only once the car was out of sight did she light another cigarette. She did not bother to move from her position, instead staying there until Dalton came back. He sat down on the swing and did not say anything for several minutes. Lydia waited for him to start the conversation.

"It has been five year since I have a drink," Dalton said, "And today I wish there was one in my hand."

"You can go find one," Lydia said.

"No," Dalton said, "A drink might count as marks against me the next time I am in court."

"You an alcoholic and not tell anyone?" Lydia asked, "Because if you are I think you might have missed one of the twelve steps."

"No, but you think Megan is going to let a drink slip by her radar," Dalton said, "She can make one drink sound like a two year binge."

"She can make sugar sound like you are popping cyanide," Lydia said, "But common sense tells one otherwise."

"It is the pause between when her persuasive voice stops and common sense kicks in that can stretch to several hours," Dalton said, "And apparently she found herself a job."

"Doing what? Beating people who think about eating sugar, wheat, or dairy?" Lydia asked.

"The job title is personal trainer," Dalton said answered.

"Who would be stupid enough to want her as a personal trainer?" Lydia asked.

"Some gym hired her to help their clients," Dalton answered, "So, the people themselves aren't picking her, they just get to work with whoever is available."

"Poor them," Lydia said.

The ping of a text sounded. Dalton started feeling for his phone, but stopped when Lydia pulled out her phone. She checked the text.

"When did you get a phone?" Dalton asked.

"When Robert got worse," Lydia answered, "I wanted the doctor to be able to get in touch with me if Robert got worse when I wasn't there. Or near the end if he died while I was off somewhere else."

"The contract isn't up yet?" Dalton asked.

"They do two year contracts these days," Lydia answered, "You're supposed to be paying off the cost of the phone as part of the monthly fee and right now it would cost more to break the contract than keep the phone."

"Who has the number to be able to text you?" Dalton asked, "Because I doubt the doctor still keeps in touch."

"He phones when he wants to talk to me," Lydia said, "This text is from Alicia."

"And what did she have to say?" Dalton asked.

"Hi," Lydia answered.

"I shouldn't have bothered to ask, should I have?"

"You know the answer to that."

"I can't believe you told Caitlyn that you are a thief."

"I was supposed to lie to her?"

"You lie about it to most everyone else."

"Caitlyn was asking why you lied to her classmates, which led to a discussion about what I did for a job. She called me on my vague answers. I asked what you had said and she told me that she was supposed to ask me. So, I told her."

"I hope there were some warning labels applied."

"We agreed stealing was bad and I told her not to do it. I said that as an adult I could do things she wasn't allowed to do. She didn't like my logic, but accepted it. We haven't talked about since. How did your conversation with her go about me taking her from her mother?"

Dalton sighed and ran his hand through his hair. He barely let the air refill his lungs before he sighed again.

"Always good to know things can go that well," Lydia said, "At least she won't be asking me for a while."

"I tried to explain to her that we hadn't won on the way home," Dalton said, "But she was just so happy to coming home and ignoring what I had to say. She is going to be very disappointed when Megan tries again for custody and might actually succeed."

"You have a lot of work ahead of you," Lydia said.

"And you're gone in two and a half weeks," Dalton said.

"I wasn't staying forever," Lydia said, "If you want a mother figure for Caitlyn, who isn't Megan, you have to find yourself a girlfriend."

"Dating someone for the sole purpose of getting a mother for your child is not the proper way to date," Dalton said, "You start out looking for someone you like and then let the relationship build to the point of introducing them to your child. If you want a nanny or a babysitter, it is better to hire one."

"That is probably a healthy way to look at things," Lydia said.

"Probably?" Dalton asked with a raised eyebrow.

"I don't define my relationships by whether they like my child or not," Lydia answered, "I don't know how dating works once you add children into the mix. I barely know how dating works."

"That explains most of your relationships," Dalton said, "Though Robert seemed good for you."

"Robert would have been a longer term relationship," Lydia said, "But it ended too soon."

"I have some work that I can from home," Dalton said as he got up.

"You picking up Caitlyn or am I?" Lydia asked.

"I'll give you a break today and get her," Dalton answered, "After all we wouldn't want you to get too domesticated."

"Good idea," Lydia said.

Dalton went inside. Lydia lit another cigarette.

Because Dalton was there and Caitlyn was doing better, Lydia left earlier. She reached the bar before McKing and sat down at her usual table. The bar was still filling up. The bartender came and delivered Lydia's drink. There was also a folded piece of paper along with it. The bartender went back to his position behind the bar. Lydia looked at the writing on the piece of paper before tucking it away.

Lydia was on to her second drink when McKing arrived and made his way to the table where Lydia was sitting. He stopped a server and ordered his beer.

"You're early," McKing said once the server had moved on.

"I wasn't needed at home," Lydia replied, "Dalton got custody and everything is fine for the moment."

"Good," McKing said.

"You have an information broker?" Lydia asked.

"Yes," McKing's tone was hesitant.

"Do you think you get them to look up Megan Porter, currently Megan Sumeton?" Lydia asked.

"What are you hoping to find?" McKing asked.

"Anything that will make her back off," Lydia answered.

"Why don't you ask Dalton about her?" McKing asked.

"He quit paying attention to her a few years ago," Lydia answered, "And he never bothered to find out much of her history before they married. He felt it rude to check out someone and that you should wait for them to talk to you."

"Well, he isn't wrong," McKing said, "But he reached the wrong conclusion about it. If they don't tell you anything, don't marry them. Though if he quit paying attention to her, I don't blame her for finding herself meeting those needs outside the relationship."

"I don't claim his response to the situation was a good one, but his attention drifted to work about the time she was getting into veganism and stuff about vibes," Lydia said, "She seemed normal when they married and when Caitlyn was born, but then she turned into one of those freaky people who has decided the best way to live and if you don't agree with her than you are wrong about everything. She got into a fight with her boytoy because he had beer to drink one night."

"I can ask," McKing said, "But don't expect much."

"I don't," Lydia said, "I'm just trying what I know."

"I finally heard back from my sources on Justin," McKing said, "His story checks out on the surface, but once you get a couple layers deeper not so much. I can't confirm he is an undercover cop, but there are some things suggesting such. I have someone else I can suggest for the Friday job."

"You got the rest of the information for the Friday job?" Lydia asked.

"Yeah," McKing took some paper out of his pocket and slid them across the table to her, "All the information on the building that I can get."

Lydia took the papers and looked through them. The server brought McKing's beer and Lydia's third drink. Finally, Lydia folded the papers up and put them into her pocket.

"Okay," Lydia said, "Two necessary, three best. Call Justin and get him for the Friday job."

"Why?" McKing asked, "I just told you what he is."

"What is the word on the street about Stevenson?" Lydia asked.

"He is still looking for information on the woman in the picture who someone identified as a participant of the Houdini Challenge," McKing said, "Justin isn't going to protect you from him."

"No, but the further I get into this adoption thing the more I think having an undercover cop along would be a good thing," Lydia said, "And he is going to get suspicious if the only jobs he gets invited along to help out with are related to one specific thing. By inviting him to other jobs, it makes it seem like we trust him."

"You make a good argument," McKing said, "But you are giving him more information about you and you are more likely to be caught."

"I'm not sticking around," Lydia said, "Once the Houdini Challenge starts, I will be off and I don't plan to come back."

"Even to visit?" McKing asked.

"Well, maybe a yearly visit to see Caitlyn," Lydia answered, "But even that is not certain. You're the one who might get into trouble."

"I've already working with him on several jobs," McKing said, "And introduced him around. I don't think I am getting out of this unless I find some reason for him not to arrest me."

"Save his life?"

"From what? None of the jobs I take are dangerous."

"Convince him you haven't done anything wrong."

"You have met him. He isn't that stupid."

"How's Felicia?"

"Today she seemed more distant and I couldn't get any answers as she wouldn't talk about it. I don't know if it is one of those things she just refuses to talk about with me or whether it is a current issue and she isn't ready to tell me."

"Hopefully she just isn't ready to tell you."

"I thought I knew Felicia, but I talk to her and I wonder."

"You know her well enough to distinguish between the two. I would say you're up on most guys there."

"You keep putting positive spins on the thoughts eating away at me."

"You are over thinking things. Quit trying to analysis everything she says, instead spent this time getting to know her all over again. Learn who she is now. You have both grown and changed since you met, as much as you don't think so. She needs to learn about you and you need to learn about her."

"Where is this all coming from?"

"Wisdom comes from experience and overthinking things when the person you love goes into the ground rather than stays in your arms."

"I'll just come to you for that wisdom, rather than have the experience."

"That is the preferred method."

The server brought fresh drinks for both of them. The bartender gave up his position and headed into the back.

"I'll be back," Lydia said before getting up. She went into the back. The bartender had left the back door open a crack. Lydia went out and made sure it did not close behind her. The bartender was sitting on a garbage can and lighting his cigarette. Lydia took the garbage can across from him.

"Give them up?" the bartender lifted his cigarette briefly.

"No," Lydia answered, "Just don't feel like on right now. The note said you wanted to talk."

"Yeah, I'm not sure who to go to about this," the bartender said, "It has to do with my sister. Since she and her last boyfriend broke up, she has been crashing at my place. She spent the first week drinking herself to sleep. Then she started going out again, which I took for a good sign. Then she started disappearing for days at a time, which didn't really bother me because I'm used to living alone and I was really hoping she was finding a life for herself separate from mine. Then the other day I found this."

The bartender pulled a note out of his pocket and offered it to Lydia.

"Pay the twenty thousand you owe or something bad will happen," Lydia read.

"I asked her about it," the bartender said, "But she tried to laugh it off. The assurances that sound false and you know they are false, but the person telling them won't change their stance. Then I found this in my mailbox."

The bartender took about paper out of his pocket and handed it to Lydia.

"If you want your sister back pay us twenty thousand," Lydia said.

"I checked out the address on my way to work this evening," the bartender said, "It was one of those abandoned houses out on Monty Road. Looked like no one had been there in a long time. I didn't stop to check it out so that is just my impression as I went by."

"Your sister ever talk about the people she was hanging out with?" Lydia asked.

"She mentioned a Matt," the bartender said, "But she never said who he was or what their relationship was. I don't remember her naming anyone else."

"And you don't want to go to the police?" Lydia asked.

"I didn't notice that she hasn't been around for the last couple days," the bartender said, "I don't know anything about her activities. I don't have anything except a ransom note."

"Since I assume you don't have the ransom. Do you have a picture of your sister?" Lydia asked.

"Yeah, Sara Alban" the bartender took out his wallet and pulled out a picture, which he handed to Lydia, "Twenty thousand is most of a year's salary and I don't save up much as it all goes to rent and food. You got twenty thousand lying around for a loan?"

"No," Lydia answered, "Twenty thousand would require several big jobs and this seems like a limited time offer."

"Can you help me find her?" the bartender asked, "I really don't know what else to do."

"I can look into it and see what I can find," Lydia said.

"I would greatly appreciate it," the bartender said.

"I'm going to recruit a local to help me," Lydia said, "Hopefully we can find something out before you head home."

"Thanks," the bartender said.

Lydia nodded before going back inside the bar. She went through the back room and entered the bar itself. McKing was still sitting at the table sipping his beer. Lydia sat back down on her seat.

"What was that about?" McKing asked.

"The bartender was looking for some help," Lydia answered, "And since he does me favours, I figure I owe him. I was also hoping you can help me."

"You wouldn't let me break into places the other day," McKing said.

"I am hoping this doesn't involve breaking into places," Lydia said, "And if it does, you can wait in the car. Mostly it involves knowing the locals."

"Let's hear it," McKing said.

"Girl has gone missing," Lydia said, "She was drinking heavily and then starting going out places. She met up with some guy named Matt and there was an unexplained note about her owing twenty thousand but to whom is not known. The twenty thousand is supposed to be dropped off at a house on Monty Road."

"You're talking Matthew Halbert," McKing said, "He owns Monty Road."

"What are his vices?" Lydia asked.

"Gambling," McKing answered.

"Anything else?" Lydia asked.

"Is there more to this girl's disappearance than you are telling me?" McKing asked.

"The ransom note," Lydia answered, "Which her family member can't afford to pay."

"Either he is getting sloppy," McKing said, "Or someone else is the real problem."

"How does one get an audience with Matthew Halbert?" Lydia asked.

"Offer to join his poker game," McKing answered.

"I better off picking his pocket or rifling through his office," Lydia said.

"Not sure those options will get you what you want in this case," McKing said, "We can go and see if he'll talk to us. Since we aren't doing anything illegal, I don't have to wait in the car."

"Let's go," Lydia said flagging down the server.

Once they had settled up, they went out to McKing's car. McKing drove through the city streets to a club and parked in the only space he could find, which was the alley across the street. Neither Lydia or

McKing matched those who stood in line waiting to be let in. As if to enforce the matter, the doorman looked them over and frowned.

"We were wondering if we could talk to Matt," McKing said.

"Got an appointment?" the doorman asked.

"Nope," McKing answered, "But we were hoping to talk to him anyway."

"And you would be?" the doorman asked.

"Neal," McKing answered.

The doorman gave McKing a look of expectant dismissal but went to the man inside the door to have the message delivered.

"You on first name basis?" Lydia asked.

"No," McKing answered, "But I am hoping he recognizes the name and is curious as to what I want."

"I hope it works," Lydia said.

They waited several minutes as the doorman continued his work. Then another man stepped outside and nodded to the doorman.

"Apparently Matt is bored this evening," the doorman told McKing, "Follow Deven."

"Thank you," McKing said. He and Lydia followed the other man inside. He took them around the thumping dance floor and the booths where people were drinking. The music made it impossible to hear anything and the people were yelling at each other anyway. The place was not filled to capacity, but it was a Wednesday night.

Deven reached a door on the other side of the place. He used a key to open it. McKing and Lydia followed him inside. Once the door was closed behind them the noise dropped to the point of being able to hear someone talk. They went down a hallway to a back room. This room had some stock pushed back against the walls, but the main point in the room was the table with four men playing poker. Deven whispered in one man's ear and then left. The man had a bigger presence than the other three, though he was the same size.

"McKing," the man said without taking his attention away from the poker game, "Come to join the game?"

"No, Matt," McKing answered.

"How about your friend?" Matt asked.

"I lose at solitaire," Lydia answered. Matt chuckled.

"So, what brings you to my den?" Matt asked.

"Looking for Sara Alban," Lydia answered.

"That would make three of us," Matt said, "I've been expecting her to come join to the table for a couple days now and she hasn't showed."

"She owe you money?" Lydia asked.

"No," Matt turned his attention to Lydia, "Why are you asking that question?"

"She had a note saying she owed someone twenty thousand," Lydia said, "And then she disappeared."

"I don't know anything about her owing anyone money," Matt said, "She was on a winning streak. She collected ten thousand a night at this table for several nights."

"And you were still letting her play?" Lydia raised an eyebrow at him.

"It wasn't just my money," Matt chuckled, "But I understand your implication. The answer is yes."

"Then maybe they delivered this to the wrong address," Lydia said taking out a paper and offering it to Matt. He took it and read it through the glasses sitting on his nose. The area around him went from cautious but non-threatening to just short of anger.

"Who was it delivered to?" Matt asked.

"Her brother," Lydia answered, "And he doesn't have the money."

"That is Calder's place," Matt said, "But I don't see him being this stupid."

"He's been low on money lately," the man beside Matt spoke up. The game had come around to Matt and it stopped the play leaving everyone waiting for Matt.

"Maybe he thinks he'll get a cut if he helps out," the man on the other side of Matt said.

"That makes more of Calder's sense," Matt said, "If I give you the twenty thousand, can you try to bring it back? I'll send Deven if you need."

"Does he know anything about escalation and ways to avoid it?" Lydia asked.

"He isn't a mindless minion," Matt answered, "And Calder knows him, which might make everything easier."

"Fine," Lydia said.

"I only ask you bring me the name of the person who is responsible for this," Matt said.

"We'll try," Lydia said. Matt nodded.

"Deven," Matt called as he turned his attention back to the game. Deven came back from the hallway.

"Go with McKing and his friend," Matt said, "After you take twenty thousand dollars from the office. Don't do anything stupid as it will endanger people."

"Yes, sir," Deven said. Then he went to the door on the far side of the poker table.

"Visiting our fair city?" Matt asked Lydia while still paying attention to the game.

"For a short while," Lydia answered.

"You work with McKing?" Matt asked.

"Same field," Lydia answered, "Occasionally we work together."

"Know a man named Kenley?" Matt asked.

"Any reason for asking?" Lydia replied.

"He's my brother," Matt said, "And I haven't heard anything about him in years."

"Why don't you just phone him?" Lydia asked.

"Don't have his number," Matt answered.

"Pity," Lydia said. Matt looked at Lydia over his glasses, but her face gave away nothing. Before Matt could ask any more questions, Deven came back with a bag. He gave it to Lydia and then the three went into the hallway. Once back into the club, Deven led the way back to the front door.

Outside the club, McKing took the lead. They went back to McKing's car. McKing went to open the driver's side, but Deven stopped him.

"I'll drive," Deven said.

"It is my car," McKing said.

"You've been drinking," Deven said, "I can smell the beer on your breath."

"Just let him," Lydia said as she moved to the back door. McKing appeared to want to argue the point, but instead he shrugged and went around to the passenger side.

"Calder's place on Monty Road," McKing said once they were all buckled up.

Deven started the engine and pulled out of the parking spot. Once on the road, he drove as if he knew exactly where they were going, which Lydia assumed he did. Without speeding, Deven got them to the house on Monty Road in a short amount of time.

The house looked like it had been abandoned. There were no lights and no maintenance.

"I have flashlights in the trunk," McKing said.

They got out of the car and went around back, where McKing opened the trunk and dug through the stuff for the flashlights. He gave one each to Deven and Lydia. He kept one for himself before shutting the trunk. They turned them on before going up the walk to the house. Deven reached the door first and pushed it open. Lydia and McKing followed him inside. They entered a hallway running the length of the house with stairs going up from there and doorways on either side.

Deven went to the left, which had at one time been a living room. The only piece of furniture left was the couch and there was someone stretched out on it. His eyes were closed and he was breathing. He also was wearing clothes too good for his surroundings.

"Calder," Deven's voice was loud in the room. The man twitched and then slowly opened his eyes. He looked at Deven and then Lydia and finally McKing. Calder sat up.

"What is this?" Calder asked.

"You know who sent a ransom note for Sara Alban?" Lydia asked, "Because this is the address they said to leave the money."

"I haven't been here in a week," Calder said, "I was out of town with work. I wasn't supposed to be back for another few days."

"Seen any signs that another person has been here?" Deven asked.

"I wasn't looking for any on my way in," Calder answered, "I was tired and assumed no one would bother."

"Mind if we look around?" Deven said.

"Go ahead," Calder said as he leaned back. Lydia and McKing headed back into the hallway while Deven went to the other doorway in the living room. There was little to show someone lived in the house. Most of the furniture was gone and what was left did not look usable. The upstairs was in the same condition. Nowhere did there appear to be any disturbance in the last week or month. They went back down to the living room, where Calder had not moved from the couch.

"Nothing here," Deven said.

"I could've-" Calder started.

"Shut off the flashlights," Lydia whispered. McKing and Lydia did it at the same time with Deven following their example. They stood without speaking. There were the sounds of tires on gravel coming from behind the house.

"There is an alley way back there," Calder whispered, "And a gate."

"Any sheds or buildings they can hide someone?" Lydia asked.

"Nope," Calder answered, "Just an outside entrance to the basement."

"I checked the basement," Deven whispered, "No one has been down there." He moved to stand with his back to the wall beside the doorway.

The vehicle stopped and a door was closed. The back gate creaked. There was a long stretch of quiet as they made their way across the lawn. Then the back door opened. Footsteps came down the hallway and the man stepped into the living room. McKing turned on his flashlight right in the face of the man. The man brought his hand up to shade his eyes from the glare.

"David?" Calder asked.

"I thought you weren't home for another couple days," David said.

"I came home early," Calder said, "What are you doing here?"

"Well, I needed some place to crash for the night," David said.

"You drove here to sleep here?" Calder asked.

"I can see this is not a good place to be," David turned to leave, but Deven had moved into the doorway and blocked his exit.

"These people are looking for someone stupid enough to demand a ransom for Sara Alban," Calder said, "You wouldn't be that stupid? And use my house as the drop-off?"

"Of course not," David chuckled in such a way as to suggest that was exactly why he was there. He turned back to Calder.

"She owe you money?" Lydia asked.

"What?" David asked looking at her in confusion.

"Then what was with the message about the debt of twenty thousand?" Lydia asked, "The same amount you are asking for the return of Sara."

"I don't know what you are talking about," David answered in the tone of voice suggesting he was lying.

"David bets on sports games," Calder said, "Sometimes he gets in too deep and then has to figure out how to dig himself out again. But this time, he should have kept betting until he got a big one to pay some of those debts."

"So, that leaves us with a couple problems," Lydia said, "The first being where Sara is and the second is to what to tell Matt since he wanted to know who would be stupid enough to demand a ransom for her."

"This isn't about Matt," David said.

"It is now," Deven said.

"But she said she had a brother," David said.

"Who can't afford such a ransom," Lydia said.

"But she said that was where she got the money," David said.

"Of course, she did," Lydia said, "As a single female, you don't tell a man that you have money. That is just foolishness."

"Where is she?" Deven asked, "We can do this the easy way or the hard way."

"I'll tell you if you don't tell Matt it was me," David said.

"You passed that point," Lydia said, "It is a question of how much damage you want done to you."

"She is in the first house in this row," David said.

"And you drove here?" McKing asked.

"I wasn't planning to stick around," David said in a tone suggested such an action would be foolish.

"Deven, you want to take the money and David to back to Matt," Lydia said, "McKing and I will go get Sara and make sure she doesn't need medical help."

"Okay," Deven said, "Where is the money?"

"In the car," Lydia said, "I didn't think we would actually need to leave it here."

"I'm gonna stay here and sleep," Calder said, "Unless I'm needed for something."

"If you are, I'm sure Matt will send for you," Deven said grabbing David by the neck of his shirt and dragging him towards the front door. Lydia and McKing followed them out. Lydia got the money out of the back for Deven. David pointed to the house then Deven dragged him around to the back of the house. Lydia and McKing started down the street.

"Got information from the broker?" Lydia asked.

"Not yet," McKing answered, "He'll let me know if he has anything in the next few days."

"Friday?" Lydia asked.

"Maybe," McKing answered, "But that will be the earliest."

"You expecting a before and after on Friday?" Lydia asked.

"Yes," McKing answered.

"Figures," Lydia said.

They reached the house and went up the walkway. It had a similarly abandoned feel as Calder's house did. McKing pushed the door and it opened. Both turned on their flashlights before stepping inside. This house had a similar layout but in reverse. McKing went left and Lydia went right. They checked the main floor without finding anything. McKing went down and made sure the basement was clear while Lydia waited in the kitchen.

Then they went upstairs. In the first bedroom, they found Sara tied up in a corner. Lydia slowly moved towards her while McKing stayed in the doorway.

"Sara?" Lydia kept her voice soft. Sara nodded.

"We're going to get you out of here," Lydia said reaching Sara. She put her flashlight down and pulled out a knife. Lydia cut the ropes holding Sara as well as the gag.

'Thank you," Sara's voice was hoarse from disuse.

"Can you walk?" Lydia asked as she put the knife away.

"I think so," Sara said.

"Take it slow," Lydia said. She picked up the flashlight and stood up. Lydia held out a hand. Sara accepted the help to get to her feet. Her muscles were cramped based on how she was walking, but otherwise she was doing okay. McKing moved out of the doorway and into the hallway to let them pass. The three of them made their way out of the house. Once outside, Lydia sent McKing to get the car while she and Sara sat on the steps of the house.

"How did you find me?" Sara asked.

"David told us when he thought he was going to be picking up the ransom," Lydia answered, "He thought he could get twenty thousand out of your brother."

"My brother doesn't have that kind of money," Sara said, "I just told David that to get him to leave me alone. He tried to blackmail me because he found out some of my past, but I thought about it and realized it was nothing to be ashamed of. Does Matt know what happened?"

"He knows part of it," Lydia answered, "He'll know the rest soon enough. David is going to tell him."

"I would feel bad about that," Sara said, "But not after what he did to me."

"If you are okay with it, I thought it might be best to take you to a clinic," Lydia said, "Just to make sure you are already."

"I guess it is okay," Sara said, "He didn't do anything like that."

"Sometimes bruises hide more serious wounds," Lydia said.

"Okay," Sara said.

McKing parked the car in front of the gate. Lydia helped Sara up and they went to the car. McKing drove to a clinic and Sara was taken in to see the doctor. Lydia went outside. She took out her phone and dialed a number.

"McGregory's Corner?" the voice of the bartender came through despite the noise of the patrons in the background.

"Found her," Lydia said, "She is okay."

"Thank you," the bartender said.

"Don't know where she'll want to go from here," Lydia said.

"Just ask her to check in with me tomorrow," the bartender said.

"I will," Lydia said.

"Thank you," the bartender said.

Lydia ended the call and went back inside the clinic. She sat with McKing as they waited for the doctor to finish.

"I need to find an actual job," Lydia said, "All these cut rate and pro bono working is starting to get to me."

"Friday is an actual job," McKing said.

"But it is yours," Lydia said.

"I would like to be able to do it," McKing said, "What are you looking for?"

"I don't know," Lydia answered, "The last year to have not happened."

"They haven't invented a time machine yet," McKing said, "Though since no one from the future has shown up, it would suggest they never make one."

"You know what," Lydia said getting to her feet, "Take her wherever she wants to and tell her that her brother would like to hear from her tomorrow."

"Where are you going?" McKing asked.

"For a walk," Lydia answered.

"Are you sure that is safe?" McKing asked.

"As safe as anything else I do," Lydia answered.

"Okay," McKing said.

Lydia left the clinic. Once outside, Lydia got her bearings and started in the direction she was sure Dalton's house was.

CHAPTER SIX

"Did you get your lunch?" Dalton asked as he opened the front door and stepped out on the porch with Caitlyn following him. He turned to close the door, but stopped at the sight of Lydia sitting on the porch railing. There was no cigarette in her hand, but she was staring out into space.

"Auntie," Caitlyn said. Lydia turned to look at them.

"I thought you were still asleep," Dalton said.

"Having gotten there," Lydia said.

Caitlyn went over for a hug. Lydia hugged her back.

"What are the bruises on your arm from?" Caitlyn asked. Lydia looked down at them as if she had never seen them before.

"I bumped into something," Lydia said.

"Are you okay?" Caitlyn asked.

"Yes," Lydia answered.

"Are you sure?" Caitlyn asked.

"I am sure," Lydia answered, "Now you go and have fun at school."

"Okay," Caitlyn said. She turned to go, but stopped and looked back at Lydia. "Will you come with Dad to pick me up?"

"Sure," Lydia said. Caitlyn nodded and then turned back around. She and Dalton headed for the car. Lydia went back to her position.

Lydia came out and sat down on the railing. She lit her cigarette as the noon sun shone down. The street was quiet as everyone else was at work or school. Even the nosy neighbour had not poked her head out.

Lydia's cell rang. She took it out and pressed the button to accept the call.

"Hello?"

"This is Felicia," said the voice on the other end, "Neal's girlfriend."

"What's up?" Lydia asked.

"You were talking about a guy picking up women at a doctor's office," Felicia said.

"Yes," Lydia said.

"I think I met him this week," Felicia said, "There was this guy when I went in for my appointment. He said he was there to support his sister because her baby's father wasn't around for her. But I saw the woman he had come in with and they have no family resemblance."

"But that isn't what has you freaked out," Lydia said.

"No," Felicia said, "I was in the grocery store picking up stuff for a few days and he showed up. He gave me some reason for being there, but it was bullshit. Is he dangerous?"

"I have heard nothing about him being dangerous," Lydia said, "But none of the situations I have heard about put him in a position to act out. I would suggest you move with care. Don't agitate him. Avoid him if you can. Don't give him signals he might mispresent as interest in him."

"I will try," Felicia said, "But seeing him at the grocery store has me really freaked out."

"Did you tell the doctor about your separation with Neal?" Lydia asked.

"He said I seemed stressed," Felicia answered, "And I told him Neal and I were fighting. But I had moved out to give us both some space."

"But you didn't mention working things out," Lydia said.

"No," Felicia said, "But the doctor just suggested I limit my stress so as not to affect the baby. He didn't mention adoption or anything else, you said I should watch for."

"Have you ever seen the woman before?" Lydia asked.

"No," Felicia answered, "But I don't always see the same people while I am in his office, except for the people who work there. I heard her name though."

"You have her name?" Lydia asked.

"Sure, she was running late for her appointment," Felicia answered, "I would have thought they would have taken me in and bumped her by how late she was, but they didn't."

"If they did that, the man wouldn't have had a chance to introduce himself," Lydia said.

"That is just creepy," Felicia said.

"What were their names?" Lydia asked.

"Michael and Justine Winston," Felicia answered, "Do you think he is going to try and steal her baby?"

"Yes," Lydia answered, "And yours as well if you don't be careful."

"But she didn't look that pregnant," Felicia said, "Like maybe five months along."

"You're less than that," Lydia said, "He may feel he has the time. Most relationships take more than a couple weeks to develop, no matter how fast his technique is."

"I have to go back to the doctor," Felicia said, "The other obstetrician in town isn't taking any more patients, which is why I am going to Dr. Spencer."

"Take someone with you," Lydia said, "Can the person you are staying with go to the appointments with you?"

"Not really," Felicia answered, "She works a day job and can't take time off. We discussed it when I asked to move in for a while. If you come with me to the next one, maybe you can meet the man and it could help you with your investigation."

"If you can't find someone else to go," Lydia said, "Or I haven't managed to get him arrested."

"I can't tell Neal," Felicia said, "Yes, we have been talking and working on our relationship, but we are not at that point."

"He is going to be pissed when you get around to telling him," Lydia said, 'But it is your decision. Thank you for the information. I will see what I can with it."

"Try and get him arrested or out of the way in some from," Felicia said, "I don't want him taking my child."

"I will do what I can," Lydia said, "But I am not a problem solved. I am a thief. Phone Neal and talk to him until you calm down. I know this advice sounds rude and unnecessary, but I don't need you panicking and giving my investigation away."

"Okay," Felicia said, "I will try to be calm and I will do everything I can to avoid him."

"Thank you," Lydia said. Felicia ended the call. Lydia started searching Justine Winston on her phone. There were phone directory listings for Winstons and several social media pages dedicated to Justines. None of it was useful for Lydia's search. There were too many variables she still did not know. Lydia put her phone away and took out another cigarette. She smoked it while she thought.

As she was finishing the cigarette, Dalton's car turned on to the street. He parked it in the driveway and came up the walk.

"You gotten any sleep?" Dalton asked.

"A few hours," Lydia answered.

"Then you had a burning need for a cigarette?" Dalton asked.

"Something like that," Lydia answered.

"What happened last night?" Dalton asked.

"Nothing important," Lydia answered.

"Then why are you not willing to tell me?" Dalton asked.

"Because you don't need to know," Lydia answered.

"It looks like someone grabbed you hard enough to leave bruises," Dalton said.

"And I have no other injuries," Lydia said, "I walked home from the clinic downtown. Someone thought they deserved my attention and shortly after that discussion I was able to be on my way."

"Why did you decide to walk from downtown?" Dalton asked, "Were you looking for trouble?"

"No," Lydia answered, "I was looking for quiet. Even living with someone I have to be able to take some time to myself. Around here, it seems like there is someone around all the time."

"Did you find your quiet?" Dalton asked.

"Mostly," Lydia answered, "McKing asked me to do a job Friday night."

"Nothing around here planned to prevent you from helping him," Dalton said, "Unless you are looking for something."

"No, just telling you I'll be busy," Lydia said.

"What happened last night?" Dalton asked.

"The bartender asked me to find his sister who had been kidnapped and was being held for ransom," Lydia answered, "He was hesitant about going to the police."

"Who did it connect back to?"

"Matthew Halbert."

"Why would he be involved in a kidnapping? He makes good money running the gambling in the city."

"Someone who was in debt due to gambling thought he had found a gold mine and instead has to answer to Matthew Halbert. I got to meet Matt."

"You stay much longer and you'll know the whole underworld in the city."

"Can't stay that long."

"Probably a good thing. Matt Halbert is one of the nice ones."

"Who is Calder to Matt?"

"Why did you meet him too?"

"No, I thought I would pick out random names and see your reaction. It is a fun game. How am I doing so far?"

"Calder is to Matt as Kyle Stevenson is to Raymond Stewart."

"He is his assassin."

"I didn't say that."

"I know who Kyle Stevenson is and what he does for a living, even if I don't know who Raymond Stewart is."

"Raymond Stewart is my boss. He is also someone you do not cross in this city."

"I'll take your word for it."

"What did you do?" Dalton narrows his eyes.

"Why do you think I've done anything?" Lydia turned to look Dalton in the eye.

"Because I know that tone," Dalton said, "And I know your history."

"I have not done anything against Raymond Steward," Lydia said. Dalton sighed.

"I'm going to go polish my resume," Dalton said, "Because usually by the time you're finished not doing anything, there is little left to pick up." Dalton got to his feet and went inside.

Lydia took her phone out and brought up the internet browser. This time she typed in Raymond Stewart. Then she started going through the results.

After school, Dalton and Lydia took Caitlyn to the park with several of her friends. Dalton and the mothers stayed near the playground, while Lydia found a bench a short way away where she could watch everything. Her phone pinged and Lydia took it out to check the message. She got caught up in texted back and forth with the occasionally glance at the group on the playground.

"Dad says we should go soon," Caitlyn sat down next to Lydia. Lydia looked up at the playground and found Caitlyn's friends were headed home with their mothers. Dalton was standing there talking to a man Lydia did not recognize.

"Okay," Lydia said as she finished her text.

"What happened to your arm?" Caitlyn asked.

"Someone was trying to get my attention and he did it in the wrong way," Lydia answered.

"Did he hurt you any other place?" Caitlyn asked.

"No," Lydia answered, "I am fine."

"Why did he want your attention?" Caitlyn asked.

"Because he was being rude and I had ignored him," Lydia answered.

"He shouldn't have grabbed you," Caitlyn said, "That was wrong."

"That is true," Lydia said, "But there are people in the world who don't understand they shouldn't touch others without the person's permission. Some people are like that."

"Dad had put me in karate because of those type of people," Caitlyn said, "But Mom pulled me out because she said the instructor was giving off negative energy. But she didn't like him because he asked her to sit with the rest of the parents and not interrupt the lesson."

"Maybe we should get you back into karate," Lydia said, "Then you'll have some defense against rude people."

"I would like that," Caitlyn said, "It was fun to learn."

"Then we have to talk to your father," Lydia said.

"We have to wait until he is finished talking to that guy," Caitlyn said, "He never likes me around when he talks to that guy."

"Then I guess we wait," Lydia said, "He probably won't be too long."

They talked about what Caitlyn was learning at school while they waited.

After her late evening cigarette, Lydia went down to the bar. McKing was seated at the table. It appeared as if he was on his first beer. Lydia sat down in the chair opposite.

Before McKing could say anything, the bartender came over. He set a drink on the table for her while slipping an envelope to her under the table.

"My sister asked for me to give that to you," the bartender said.

"She okay?" Lydia asked.

"A little shaken up, but alright," the bartender answered.

"Good," Lydia said.

The bartender went back to his position behind the bar. Lydia put the envelope away.

"Pretty good job for an off the cuff," McKing said.

"What's eating you?" Lydia asked.

"I had a long conversation with Felicia," McKing said, "She was trying to calm herself after being freaked out by a guy stalking her."

"And you calmed her down?" Lydia asked.

"Of course," McKing answered, "But she won't tell me anything about the guy, so I can't actually help her."

"But you did help her," Lydia said, "You helped her calm down."

"More wisdom?" McKing asked.

"If she wanted you to help via action, she would have given you more information," Lydia said, "But all she did was want to talk."

"Still frustrating," McKing said.

"Not going to argue with that," Lydia said, "But if you expect her to take you back, you have to let her talk to you about these things when she is ready."

When the server came by, Lydia paid for her drink rather than order another one.

"Got a job tonight?" McKing asked.

"I need to break into the doctor's office again," Lydia answered.

"Need some help?" McKing asked.

"You are supposed to be going straight for Felicia," Lydia said.

"You aren't actually stealing anything," McKing said.

"And Felicia?" Lydia asked.

"You aren't saying outright no," McKing said, "Earlier this week, you would have made sure I was nowhere near this. Now, you are wavering."

"So?" Lydia asked.

"You have been talking to Felicia," McKing said.

"And you think she has changed her position?" Lydia asked, "Because I really doubt she has. It is also your decision as to whether you want to keep pursuing the straight and narrow or give it all up."

"She'll never know," McKing said, "And it is better than drinking to half-drunk before going home to an empty house. Also you aren't stealing anything."

"Breaking into the office is illegal," Lydia said, "You remember that part, right?"

"Semantics," McKing waved it off.

"Fine," Lydia said. McKing paid his tab and they left the bar. They took McKing's car.

"How is the insurance business?" Lydia asked as they were on their way.

"Boring as hell," McKing answered, "The work is boring, the co-workers are boring, and the boss is an asshole."

"Well, you knew the work was boring when you went into it," Lydia said, "The people attracted by such work probably aren't much better. As for the boss, I'm not sure what else you expected."

"I expected someone who showed respect for the people below him," McKing said, "This guy insults those below him, disappears for days at a time, and brown noses the owners into giving him raises. I sit at my desk and pretend to be an idiot. It is tiresome."

"Find something else," Lydia said, "You don't have to work at the insurance company the rest of your life. The only thing you need to make sure of is that the job is straight and there are plenty of those in this world."

"This is reminding me of elementary school," McKing said, "The teacher asking everyone what they wanted to be when we grow up."

"What was your answer back then?" Lydia asked.

"I wanted to be one of those guys on the soap opera who lives on the island and has no visible source of income," McKing answered.

"What did the teacher say?" Lydia asked.

"Not much," McKing answered, "She shook her head, offered me a book of occupations, and discussed it with my mother."

"What did your mother say?" Lydia asked.

"She said those people only exist on television," McKing answered, "Before lighting another cigarette and going back to her soap opera. I didn't think much about the question until the counsellor at high school asked me the question."

"Hoping to direct you to which college or university was best for your chosen career," Lydia said.

"I was already well developed in my career," McKing said, "The guy stuck around for several years, which was the longest my mother kept around one of the men she called my uncles. He taught me the basics and gave me my first tools of the trade. My mother didn't care as long as I shared the money with her."

"Doesn't sound like a good way to raise a child," Lydia said.

"Well, not anyway I would raise a child," McKing said, "But I didn't think it was strange at the time. Plenty of the kids I grew up with were in similar situations."

"What was the answer you gave the high school counsellor?" Lydia asked.

"I told him I was apprenticed to a car mechanic," McKing answered, "Because I was working at one to give some excuse as to where all my money could be coming from. The owner didn't care as long as I didn't sit around on my ass all day. He had a chop shop in the back to support the shop because he really didn't have enough business to keep himself open."

"So, you know cars," Lydia said.

"I knew certain aspects of cars twenty years ago," McKing said, "They are all computerized now and I haven't kept up. I can steal one if necessary, but I can't fix them."

"Customer service?" Lydia asked.

"I do enough of that at the insurance company to know I would not do well in a customer service position," McKing said.

He pulled into the unground parking for the building with the doctor's office.

"Why not take the traditional route of thieves turned straight and go into security?" Lydia asked.

"I've never been that good a thief," McKing said, "No reputation to bank on and I haven't been caught in so long people probably would assume I'm lying to pad my resume."

McKing pulled into a parking space and turned off the engine. They got out and headed for the elevator.

"What would you do if you had to go straight?" McKing asked.

"Lie," Lydia answered.

"You wouldn't go straight?" McKing asked, "Even for someone you loved."

"Last person I loved is six feet under," Lydia said, "And he never asked me to go straight even if he didn't appreciate my job. I don't see much point in changing for anyone else."

"I haven't tried to change Felicia," McKing said, "I have no idea why she is so set on changing me. I keep thinking you do, but I don't know why."

"I have no idea why either," Lydia said.

McKing used his card to bring the elevator. When the doors opened, they stepped inside.

"That is a non-answer," McKing said. Lydia shrugged.

When the doors opened, they left the elevator. Lydia unlocked the office so they could enter.

"Wait here," Lydia said.

"You don't trust me?" McKing asked.

"Not today," Lydia answered. McKing sat down in one of the chairs of the waiting room while Lydia went into the doctor's office. She started going through the files. It did not take her long to find the file she was looking for. Lydia wrote down the information she wanted. She put the file back. Then she hesitated half a second before going back through the files until she found Felicia's file. There was nothing medical stood out, but there was a post-it-note with some short-hand. Lydia copied down the note exactly as written and then put the file away.

Lydia locked up on her way out. She came out to find McKing poking around the reception desk.

"Got bored?" Lydia asked.

"Easily," McKing answered as he stepped back from the desk.

"Find anything?" Lydia asked.

"Felicia has an appointment next week," McKing answered, "Why would she be seeing a doctor so much?"

"Ask her," Lydia said.

"I can't," McKing said, "Not without telling her I helped you break into her doctor's office, which would destroy everything I have been working for."

They left the office and Lydia locked up behind them.

"What were you looking for anyway?" McKing asked.

"Contact information for someone," Lydia answered.

"I thought you got that the last time we were here," McKing said as they got into the elevator.

"I got new information and thus another person to investigate," Lydia said.

"Your investigation is going somewhere?" McKing asked.

"Things are falling into place," Lydia answered, "Still don't have a firm names or solid evidence to turn over to the police."

"Sounds like you are further along than last time we talked about it," McKing said, "Who is this next victim?"

"Justine Winston," Lydia answered.

"Never heard of her," McKing said.

"I think I know who owns the adoption agency," Lydia said, "But I'm not sure what to do about it."

"Who?" McKing said.

"Raymond Stewart," Lydia said.

"You can't do anything about Raymond Stewart," McKing said, "No one can do anything about him. He is too big."

"Not really aiming for him," Lydia said, "Just wanting to take out the adoption agency. Or at least get some babies returned to their mothers."

"Why not just aim to take out the guy selling the babies off?" McKing asked.

"He has been the hardest to pin down," Lydia answered, "The information I got this morning might help and I can probably do more to find him through my source, but I don't want to put anyone in danger."

"This sounds like it is getting complicated for a job you are going to be paid pittance for," McKing said, "I know I take on such jobs all the times because I don't worry about money as long as most of my bills get paid, but you usually don't take on so much unpaid work."

They left the elevator and walked back to the car without Lydia answering. They got into the car. McKing turned on the engine.

"It is complicated," Lydia said, "Like so many other things in my life at the moment."

"Okay," McKing said. He pulled out of the parking spot.

"Drop me off at the bar," Lydia said, "The rental car is parked near there."

McKing drove as Lydia stared out the window. He did not bother to try and talk to her. When they got close to the bar, McKing pulled the car to curb. Lydia climbed out, but before closing the door she leaned down.

"See you here tomorrow night," Lydia said.

"Have a good night," McKing said. Lydia closed the car door. She watched McKing drive off as she took out her phone. She clicked on the contact rather than put in a number. It rang a few times before someone picked up.

"What do you need?"

"I have some money to send you," Lydia said.

"Okay. Are you sure you don't want to keep some this time?"

"I have no use for it," Lydia answered, "I also got a few hundred the other day for a brief job."

"A few hundred doesn't pay the bills."

"I haven't had to pay a bill in months," Lydia said, "Everything's been paid for me."

"Good for Dalton."

"He paid my fee for the Houdini Challenge," Lydia said, "So, I'll send you this payment and you can put them with the rest."

"That would be why you are staying there for so long, but what is with the few hundred dollar job? You used to have standards."

"Since accepting Dalton's offer, they seem to have disappeared," Lydia said, "You should hear about the job I took on. Actually you probably will."

"Complete shit storm?"

"Not yet," Lydia answered, "But I've already pissed off someone who employs a mutual acquaintance."

"Considering the sort of people we both know, that is a bad thing. You gonna live through this?"

"My plan is to survive until after the Houdini Challenge," Lydia answered, "After that it doesn't matter."

"Sure it matters. Your plan might end but life does not."

"I'll send the money tomorrow," Lydia said.

"I'll expect it and put it in the right place.

"Thank you," Lydia said.

"Someday you're going to tell the whole story to someone and the world will go into shock."

"The world doesn't care about my story whether I tell it in completion or stick with half of it," Lydia said, "You just get upset because I don't tell you everything. But then again so does Dalton."

"I'm going now."

"Bye," Lydia said before hitting the button to end the call. She finished the walk back to her rental car.

CHAPTER SEVEN

Lydia had skipped her cigarette to look for the address. Now as she was driving through residential neighbourhoods, she wished she had stopped for the cigarette. This particular neighbourhood was snake like streets connecting to snake like streets. She had made several wrong turns already and was barely able to keep track of where she was.

Finally she found the street she was looking for and turn on to it. The house she was looking for was half-way down the street. She parked in front and walked up the path to the door. The lawn was taken care of and the house was as well. Lydia rang the doorbell and waiting.

It was a minute before the door opened. The woman who stood there appeared to be in her mid-sixties, but the child on her hip was maybe a year old.

"Yes?" the woman asked.

"I'm looking for Justine Winston," Lydia answered.

"You wouldn't be the only one," the woman replied, "But you won't find her here."

"Any idea where I would find her?" Lydia asked.

"I have no idea," the woman answered, "Why are you looking for her?"

"She was seen with a man who I am investigating for theft," Lydia answered.

"You aren't with the police," the woman said.

"No, I'm an independent contractor," Lydia said.

"That is a meaningless title since you could be anything," the woman said.

"I'm guessing you know nothing about Justine being with a man," Lydia said.

"She doesn't tell me anything when she is here," the woman said, "Why would she tell me anything after she decides to disappear? She has nothing to steal and we aren't giving her anything."

"She has one thing for him to steal and this would be the fourth time," Lydia said,

"He is stealing babies?" the woman asked, "Why haven't the police caught him yet?"

"No pressure from the victims," Lydia replied, "Because the victims have no idea what to do about it."

"I doubt I will see my daughter before her child is born," the woman said, "But if I do, I will call the police on the man."

"Good idea," Lydia said.

"You give up easily," the woman said.

"I'm investigating him to turn the information over to the police," Lydia said, "If you turn him over to them or information over to them, I can skip being an intermediary. All I want to for him to go to jail and the victims to get their children back."

"I'm sorry, I can't help you," the woman said.

"It didn't hurt to ask," Lydia shrugged. She headed back to her car. The woman watched Lydia take off before going back inside.

Lydia headed back to Dalton's house for her cigarette.

In the evening, Lydia parked someplace inconspicuous and then walked to the bar. This time she did not go inside. She waited between street lamps on the sidewalk. It was not long before McKing stopped next to the curb in his car. Justin was in the passenger seat. Lydia opened the back door and got in.

"Ready?" McKing asked.

"Usually," Lydia answered.

"Remember all the information?" McKing asked.

"I know the basics of what is necessary," Lydia answered, "I don't need anything else. Now are you going to keep asking questions or are we going to do this?"

"Going," McKing said. He pulled away from the curb. There was limited traffic at this time of evening, so it was quick to get out of the downtown.

"Is there a plan?" Justin asked.

"Get in, grab stuff, get out," Lydia answered.

"Lydia isn't big on planning her jobs," McKing said, "She prefers to deal with obstacles as they show up."

"Beats getting in trouble when coming across something that wasn't planned for," Lydia said.

"Just hard on anyone who needs more planning who have to work with you," McKing said.

"I thought you were staying the car," Justin said.

"He is supposed to be," Lydia said, "But he is going to follow us in in case we need a third person."

"And you're not against this?" Justin asked, "Especially after all your advice up until now."

"Felicia is coming back to him," Lydia answered, "It only a matter of time."

"How do you know?" Justin asked.

"If she tells us that it might reveal things she doesn't want anyone to know," McKing said, "I've been trying to get answers out of her since Felicia left."

"Why don't you ask Felicia?" Lydia asked, "I keep telling you to."

"Because I don't want things to go backwards with her," McKing said.

"The worst thing that could happen is she'll stop talking to you," Lydia said, "And you have already been there."

"Doesn't mean I want to go back there," McKing said.

McKing pulled into a wooded area off the side of the road. He went far enough in the car was not visible from the road, but not so far to make it hard to find. The three of them got out with their tools. McKing led the way further into the woods.

They stepped out of the woods to a narrow space between the woods and a chain link fence. They building they needed to get into was about fifty metres from the fence. There was a guard station at the gate just off the road and a guard was visible in the lit window. No other guards were visible, nor were any other kinds of security.

"There are two more guards," McKing said, "One does rounds and the other is inside."

"The fence isn't electric," Lydia said.

"It supposed to be," McKing said. Lydia pointed to the weeds growing through the fence. McKing reached out and touched the fence. Nothing happened.

"Been that way for a while," Lydia pointed to one weed which was a foot tall.

"Then we can just cut through," McKing said.

"Been a while since you were a child?" Lydia asked as she started to climb the fence. She was over and back on the ground before McKing seemed to get it. Justin followed Lydia over.

"Kids these days," McKing muttered as he gripped the metal wide to pull himself up. He took longer to get over the fence than the other two.

"Well, we know who is going to be caught if we have to run for it," Lydia said, "Which is good because I can't run."

"Then you're caught before the fence," McKing said.

"Then let's go get the items before either of us gets caught," Lydia said.

They checked around but there was nothing to worry about that moment. Then they headed across the area to the building. The area was littered with large pieces of old equipment and other junk making it easier to keep out of sight of the guard in the booth at the gate.

They stopped behind a large container with only Lydia continuing to the actual door. She worked on the lock for thirty seconds before waving the guys over. With the door open, they slipped inside. This was a reception type area with the desk for the security guards in the centre with a hallway going off each side. The guard was staring at the screens with his back to the door. McKing and Justin moved quickly and incapacitated the guard. They tied him up and rolled him under the console. Lydia went to the console and typed a few commands into the computer. When she was finished the cameras went down.

Footsteps came from the hallway to the left. Lydia ducked out of sight while Justin and McKing moved to have their backs against the walls on either side of the hallway. They waited as the footsteps got closer.

"The paper towel is running low, if you have time dur-" the other guard started as he stepped out of the hallway. Before he could do more than register the problem, McKing stepped forward and knocked him out. McKing and Justin tied the guard up before putting him with the other one.

"What now?" Justin asked.

"McKing goes right and we go left," Lydia answered, "We are after two items and once we have the item, we meet back here."

"We have until they wake up and get untied," McKing said.

"Let's move," Lydia said. She headed for the left hallway. Justin followed her while McKing headed right.

Justin caught up with Lydia. She continued passed all the doors on either side.

"Do you know where the item is?" Justin asked. Lydia took a paper out of her pocket and gave it to Justin, who looked it over. He nodded.

As they went Lydia slowed down a bit until Justin found himself walking alone. He looked back to see Lydia leaning against the wall bent over. She seemed to be in distress. He went back to her.

"What is wrong?" Justin asked.

"Can't," Lydia gasped out, "Breathe." Then she slumped down to sit on the floor. Justin knelt down. Lydia collapsed to the floor as her laboured breathing stopped. Justin moved Lydia so he could start CPR.

After two minutes, Lydia started to breathe on her own. Justin sat back. Once she was definitely breathing, Justin put her in the recovery position. Then he sat down beside her and waited.

Several minutes Lydia shifted slightly but she did not open her eyes. Her breathing was still not normal, but she did not seem to have the same trouble.

"Go get the item," Lydia said.

"What happens if you go into respiratory distress again?" Justin asked.

"Then you take the item to McKing," Lydia answered, "And you two get paid. Go."

Justin thought about it for a moment before getting up. He headed down the hallway. Lydia stayed still until his footsteps could not be heard. She took out her phone and turned it on. Once the sound let her know it was on, Lydia used one hand to write and send a text. It took several minutes before she got a response. She read it over and sent a reply. Then she put her phone back in her pocket. But Lydia did not try moving.

When she was feeling up to it, Lydia sat up and leaned against the wall. She so focused on breathing she did not notice Justin until he was kneeling beside her.

"Are you okay to get back to the car?" Justin asked.

"Help me up and we'll see," Lydia answered. Justin held out his hand. Lydia took it and used it as leverage to get up. She stayed next to the wall for a moment before she and Justin headed back toward the reception area.

They reached it to find McKing sitting at the desk waiting for them. Lydia was trying to appear okay.

"What took you so long?" McKing asked.

"Let's go," Lydia answered, "Before something else happens."

"Okay," McKing drew out the word, but he got to his feet. They left the building and went back the way they had come. When they reached the fence, Lydia went first. Only once he saw that she had made it did Justin climb over. McKing glared at the fence for a couple seconds before climbing it.

They went back through the woods and back to McKing's car. McKing opened the trunk and the items were placed there. Then they climbed into the car. Lydia buckled up before lying down on her side in the back seat.

"We can stop and drop off the cargo," McKing said, "And then we can be paid tonight."

"Drop me off at 634 Crismum on the way," Lydia said.

"Why?" McKing started the car.

"Because I asked you to," Lydia said, "And I'd breathe better if you did."

"Okay," McKing said. He drove out of the woods and turned on to the road to head back into town. There was no discussion from the front seat and Lydia did not say anything.

Ten minutes later, McKing pulled to the curb. He put the car in park and turned to the back seat.

"We're here," McKing said shaking Lydia's shoulder. She opened her eyes and slowly sat up.

"Thanks," Lydia said as she opened the car door.

"Want to be picked up once we have the money?" McKing asked.

"Sure," Lydia answered, "You'll have to wait until I come out."

"Okay," McKing said.

Lydia got out and closed the car door. She went to the building and knocked on the door. It was opened almost immediately and she went inside. Morgen closed the door behind her.

"This way," Morgen said before leading the way down a concrete hallway. They stopped at a door half-way down. This was a back door into a medical clinic. Lydia followed Morgen into one of the rooms, where Morgen had it set up for Lydia to get oxygen from a mask. Once Lydia was seated, Morgen put the mask on.

"Probably best if you stay still for fifteen minutes," Morgen said, "Dr. Warner filled me in on what you needed, but didn't tell me anything else. You can sit here for as long as you need."

"Thank you," Lydia said.

"I'll be in the office working on paperwork," Morgen said, "It is just around the corner."

Lydia nodded. Morgen left. Lydia lay down. The oxygen kept her awake and helped her feel better.

When Lydia exited the building, McKing was waiting at the curb. Lydia opened the passenger side door and got inside.

"What happened to Justin?" Lydia buckled up her seat belt.

"I decided he needed a ride home," McKing said, "Feeling better?"

"Much," Lydia answered, "But oxygen does that. Justin is definitely an undercover cop."

"Why do you say that?" McKing pulled away from the curb.

"Most thieves don't bother to stop and wait if someone is in need of CPR, let alone know how to do it," Lydia said.

"Most thieves leave you to either die or be caught," McKing said, "But that wasn't why I got rid of him."

"Why then?" Lydia said.

"My information broker got back to me on your sister-in-law," McKing said.

"Anything of actual interest?" Lydia asked.

"She is jobless," McKing answered, "Because the gym she was working for decided she didn't fit with their image. She is living in the back of a Kia Soul with a man who used to couch surf until he got together with her. The divorce has gone through as of the custody hearing, She didn't fight for any of her stuff, except what she had taken with her. The judge probably would have given her custody, but she lacked in any way to provide for her daughter."

"You haven't told me anything I don't already know," Lydia said, "Your information broker got any useful information?"

"She has been an honest citizen for the last ten years," McKing said, "Before that she had several run-ins with the law due to her career as a con-artist. She left the profession when her partner was arrested and put away for fifteen years for their last con. He refused to name her, otherwise she would have been charged as well. The police knew they worked together, but they couldn't get solid proof against her."

"Okay, that is interesting," Lydia said.

"But I don't think she is going to be a serious problem," McKing said, "From what I can tell from her history she was hoping for the child support money. She isn't going to get everything the judge requires to provide for her daughter and thus will never manage to get custody."

"You think she'll just abandon her daughter?" Lydia asked.

"I think she has done it before," McKing answered, "She had a child with a former mark and she has never even contacted them since she disappeared with some of his money."

"So, best thing to do is pay her off and let her go on her way," Lydia said.

"From her history, yes," McKing said, "But in such a way as she doesn't think she can get any more money from the same source."

"I'll talk to my brother," Lydia said.

"I'm surprised you didn't catch on to her," McKing said.

"Never spent much time around her," Lydia said, "And when I was around her I was concentrating on her daughter."

McKing pulled to the curb where he had picked up Lydia. He put the car in park before reaching into his pocket. He took out an envelope and offered it to her.

"Your pay for the evening," McKing said.

"Thank you," Lydia said, "See you around."

"Good night," McKing said.

Lydia got out of the car. After closing the door, she walked the short way down the block to her rental car. McKing had driven off.

CHAPTER EIGHT

Lydia was half-way through her morning cigarette when her cell rang. She took it out and pressed the call button.

"Yes?"

"Did you find Justine Winston?" Felicia's voice came over the line.

"No," Lydia answered, "I followed the address she gave the doctor, but it let to her parents. They don't know where she is either. Have you seen him since the other day?"

"Yes," Felicia said, "I went to pick myself up some lunch and he showed up. I saw him from a distance, so I was able to avoid him. But it is creepy. It is almost like I can't go anywhere without him showing up, but I can't stay trapped in the apartment."

"Want a suggestion?" Lydia asked.

"I'm not going to like it, am I?" Felicia asked.

"Get back together with Neal," Lydia answered, "Use him as protection against this person."

"I was hoping," Felicia started but then she stopped and was quiet for a minute, "He isn't going to change, is he?"

"I would go about extracting a promise not to teach the child the trade," Lydia said, "And avoid discussing his profession until the child understands right and wrong."

"How do you tell a child that something is wrong when an adult they know and trust does it for a living?" Felicia asked.

"With care and the right words," Lydia answered, "You have a few years to think about as most children don't come out of the womb asking about their parent's jobs. Most of what a child needs for those first couple years is love."

"Neal said you don't have children," Felicia said.

"And never will," Lydia said, "But I have a niece and many of the same lessons apply."

"Does she know what you do?" Felicia asked.

"Yes," Lydia answered, "And I have told her she shouldn't do that same. Only time will tell whether she actually listens, but I didn't portray it as anything good or something she should get into herself."

"I suppose it is all in how it is presented," Felicia said.

"Both you and Neal are smart," Lydia said, "You will figure it out. Or your child will be a really good thief."

"I'll consider that to be a poor joke," Felicia said.

"You can take it any way you want," Lydia said, "As long as you tell Neal what is going on if you expect him to help you."

"I will," Felicia said.

"Good," Lydia said.

"I suppose you'll know shortly if I did or not," Felicia said.

"The next time I talk to Neal, he'll mention it," Lydia said, "He doesn't have this number and we aren't set to meet anytime soon."

"He hasn't set up a job that needs doing?" Felicia asked.

"Did it last night," Lydia answered.

"Did Neal participate?" Felicia asked.

"Does it matter?" Lydia answered.

"I suppose not," Felicia said, "Let me know if there is anything I can do to help you with finding Justine Winston."

"I will," Lydia said. Felicia had ended the call so Lydia put her phone away.

Lydia took out her pack of cigarettes, but stared at it rather than take another cigarette out. Her phone pinged. She took it out and checked who had messaged her. Lydia put her phone away. She took a cigarette and put the rest of the pack away.

As she lit it, Dalton's car came down the street. He pulled into the driveway before both he and Caitlyn got out. They came up the walk to the porch.

"Hello, Auntie," Caitlyn said with a smile.

"Hey, Cait," Lydia said, "How are you today?"

"We have brunch and it was delicious," Caitlyn said, "And we're going to the park after this."

"Sounds like fun," Lydia said.

"Want to come?" Caitlyn asked.

"Not today," Lydia answered, "I stayed out too late last night and am still very tired. Maybe another day."

"Okay," Caitlyn said. She went into the house slightly disappointed.

"What is wrong?" Dalton asked.

"Just tired," Lydia answered, "But I did learn something last night you might be interested in."

"What is that?" Dalton asked.

"Someone was suggesting that based on Megan's history, if you offer some money while making sure she knows she can't get more out of you, she'll disappear," Lydia answered.

"Do I want to know about the history referred to?" Dalton asked.

"I can tell you," Lydia said.

"No, I don't want to know," Dalton said, "I'll talk to my attorney later."

"Where's my water bottle?" Caitlyn called from inside the house.

"I'm coming," Dalton called back before going into the house.

Lydia sat there and finished her cigarette. Once Dalton and Caitlyn had what they needed, they left for the park. Lydia watched them go. When she was ready, Lydia went to her rental car.

She drove downtown and parked in a pay lot with enough it the meter for the whole afternoon. Then Lydia walked to the clinic from yesterday. It was open and she was able to go right in. The receptionist was seated behind the desk and looked up at her.

"Can I help you?" the receptionist asked.

"I was hoping Morgen had some time to see me," Lydia answered.

"Dr. Kresh is busy today," the receptionist said, "But there may be some time when she can fit you in."

"Thank you," Lydia said.

"Your name?" the receptionist asked.

"Lydia Sumeton."

"Have you seen Dr. Kresh before?" the receptionist asked.

"I was referred to her by Dr. Warner," Lydia said.

"Have a seat and I'll let you know when you can see Dr. Kresh," the receptionist said.

Lydia nodded before turning around and taking a seat. She leaned her head against the wall and waited. The receptionist went back to working.

Other patients came in and were taken back to examining rooms. Some came with family members who sat and waited. After an hour or so of Lydia being there a young woman who had come in with an elderly lady approached the desk.

"Yes?" the receptionist asked.

"The woman in the corner," the young woman said pointing at Lydia, "I don't think she is breathing."

The receptionist got up and came around the desk. She went over to Lydia. Lydia was breathing shallowly, but not well. The receptionist headed to the area of the examining rooms. Morgen was just finishing with a patient and exiting the room.

"Yes?" Morgen asked when she saw the receptionist.

"A woman came in asking to see you," the receptionist said, "I said I would fit her in when I could and now she is having trouble breathing."

"Lydia," Morgen said.

"That was what she said her name was," the receptionist said.

"We need to get her into examining room two," Morgen said, "She needs to be on oxygen immediately."

The receptionist went back out the waiting area and over to Lydia. She started shaking Lydia's shoulder. Lydia did not immediately respond, but finally she opened her eyes.

"Come on," the receptionist said, "Morgen says to get you to examining room two."

"Okay," Lydia's words were breathless as she tried to get to her feet. The receptionist helped Lydia up and towards the examining room. When they reached the hallway, Morgen came and put Lydia's arm over her shoulder to help them. This was good because Lydia was not holding up well. They reached the examining room and got Lydia on to the table. Morgen put the oxygen mask on Lydia while the receptionist went back out to her desk.

"I am sorry," Morgen said as she checked Lydia over, "I forgot to give her instructions to bring you in here immediately if you showed up. However, needing oxygen twice in two days suggests your condition is getting worse."

"Dr. Warner sent you my file," Lydia said.

"He thought it was necessary if you were going to come to me," Morgen said, "Especially since he has been very worried about how you were doing since you didn't appear to have searched out any medical help."

"Aside from a few attacks I haven't needed any," Lydia said, "And they came on suddenly. But today I was tired, so I thought I should find some help before I was in trouble. Or at least I thought I was."

"Dr. Warner said you were likely to refuse to do more tests," Morgen said, "But if I did them, we would know how far you condition had deteriorated since Dr. Warner did them. This will tell you how often you need oxygen and how bad your next attack will likely be."

"You want to do uncomfortable things so you can track how fast I am dying," Lydia said, "And the answer is no. If I wanted to feel like someone science experiment, I would have stuck around Dr. Warner."

"I'm guessing you haven't implemented any of Dr. Warner's suggestions," Morgen said, "Like quitting smoking."

"It is easier on my nerves to keep smoking," Lydia said.

"The cigarettes are making things worse for you," Morgen said, "Shortening you're already shortened life."

"As long as I survive the next month and a half, I don't care," Lydia said.

"Cut down to one a day if you can," Morgen said, "Or two at most to make sure you reach that goal."

"I will try," Lydia said.

"I will leave instructions with my receptionist that you are to be brought in here as soon as you arrive," Morgen said, "So, you can come in when you need to."

"Thank you," Lydia said.

"You can go when you are up to it," Morgen said, "There is no rush."

Lydia nodded. Morgen left the examining room and closed the door behind her. Lydia closed her eyes and let the world settle.

Lydia blinked herself back into the world. The clock said a couple hours had past. She lifted the mask off her face and sat up. She was feeling much better than when she had woken up. Lydia got off the examining table and went the door. There was no one in the hallway, but the doors to the other examining rooms were open, except one. Lydia went back out to the waiting area. The receptionist looked up for her desk.

"I am sorry about what happened," the receptionist said, "Dr. Kresh told me to let you go straight in when you come in."

"At least I'm okay for today," Lydia said. She left the clinic.

As Lydia was walking to the parking lot where she left her rental car, her phone pinged. She took it out and checked the text messages. There were two from earlier she had not heard while she was in the clinic and then another one. She put her phone away without answering the messages.

Lydia got back to her car. There was still half an hour on the ticket. Lydia got in and was about to start the car when her phone rang. She took it out and pressed the button.

"Are you trying to ignore me?" the voice on the other end did not wait for her to say hello.

"The person you are trying to reach is unavailable at this time. Leave a message after the tone."

"You sent me money today."

Lydia did not respond.

"Do you want me to do with it the same as the rest?"

"No, I sent it to you because I got tired of burning it myself."

"Bank transfers are hard to ignite."

"And how is that my problem?"

"We need to talk."

"Also not my problem. I have things to do. Bye."

"Lydia!"

Lydia pressed the button to end the call. She put her phone away and started the car. She ignored the ringtone as well as the pings to announce the text messages.

Lydia parked in her spot in front of Dalton's house and got out. Dalton's car was in the driveway, but she could not hear anyone making noise from the backyard. Lydia went inside. She found Dalton and Caitlyn sitting at the kitchen table with colouring supplies and snacks. Caitlyn looked up from her picture.

"Hi, Auntie," Caitlyn said.

"Hello, Cait," Lydia said as she got herself a glass of water, "How are things here?"

"It was lots of fun at the park, but then it started to rain," Caitlyn said. Lydia sat down at the table away from the projects.

"You look better," Dalton said.

"I feel better," Lydia said.

"Maybe you can join us for our next activity," Caitlyn said.

"And what is that?" Lydia asked.

"We were going out back to kick around the soccer ball," Dalton answered, "We were just waiting for the weather to clear."

"I am willing to go out and watch you," Lydia said, "But I can't play soccer."

"My teacher says if we aren't good at something, we just need to practice," Caitlyn said, "And that there is nothing we can't do."

"Your teacher is right with certain exceptions," Lydia said, "Those exceptions are when your body is not able to do something. You can practice to get better at soccer, while I can't practice at all. "

"Does this have something to do with when you collapsed at the ice cream shop?" Caitlyn asked.

"Yes," Lydia answered.

"But you hadn't played any games," Caitlyn said.

"Sometimes I don't have to," Lydia replied, "Sometimes the oxygen in my blood gets too low and without oxygen the body doesn't function well."

"That is usually a sign of serious illness," Dalton said.

"Are you sick, Auntie?" Caitlyn looked at Lydia with deeply concerned eyes.

"What are you colouring?" Lydia asked looking at the picture in front of Caitlyn. Caitlyn looked down at the picture as well.

"It is a parrot," Caitlyn said, "Brenton in my class was allowed to bring his for show and tell. His dad brought it for show and tell and then took it home because it wasn't allowed to stay." Caitlyn went back to colouring. The look Dalton gave Lydia suggested he was not so easily distracted.

"Brenton has two dads," Caitlyn said, "Apparently they are gay."

"It would be a really awkward situation if they were living together like that and weren't," Lydia said.

"What?" Caitlyn looked up for her colouring with a confused look.

"Your aunt was making a joke," Dalton said.

"More of an observation," Lydia said, "So, you liked the parrot?"

"It was fun," Caitlyn answered, "The parrot could talk and was pretty colours. But I wouldn't want one."

"Why not?" Lydia asked.

"They poop all over the place," Caitlyn answered.

"Good reason," Lydia said.

"Did you ever have a pet when you were little?" Caitlyn asked.

"Nope," Lydia answered.

"Why not?" Caitlyn asked.

"Why don't you have a pet now?" Lydia asked.

"Mom didn't want one," Caitlyn answered.

"We never talked about it," Dalton said, "But the reason you don't have any pets is that I am allergic to fur. That is also why your aunt never had pets."

"Did you want one?" Caitlyn asked.

"No," Lydia answered, "I've never been much of an animal person. It was Alicia who would go next door to play with their dogs."

"Who is Alicia?" Caitlyn asked.

"She is your other aunt," Lydia answered, "You have never met her because she has a very busy life and doesn't get to visit."

"Does she have any children?" Caitlyn asked.

"She isn't married," Lydia answered.

"Does a person have to be married to have children?" Caitlyn asked.

"She said she would never have children until after she was married," Lydia answered, "But there are plenty of people who have children without being married. It is a matter of choice for some people and mistakes for others."

"Dad, was I a choice or a mistake?" Caitlyn asked.

"You were a choice," Dalton answered.

"Is choice why you don't have children, Auntie?" Caitlyn asked.

"Yes," Lydia answered.

"I think the weather has cleared up enough we can go outside," Dalton said.

"Okay," Caitlyn said, "I'll finish my parrot later."

The three of them put on their shoes and went out back. Lydia settled on the deck and watched the other two play.

When Dalton took Caitlyn up to tuck her into bed, Lydia went outside to sit on the railing of the front porch. She did not take out a cigarette. Instead she took out her phone. She pressed the contact to call the person and then put the phone to her ear. It rang several times before the person answered.

"Hello?" McKing said.

"Got a number for Justin?" Lydia asked, "I need his help with the baby investigation."

"Sure," McKing said before giving Lydia seven numbers.

"Thanks," Lydia said.

"Felicia called me today," McKing's tone was hard to read.

"This is a good thing, right?" Lydia asked.

"I'm not sure yet," McKing answered, "She wants to move back in, but not back into our bedroom. I might have said no, but she sounded scared."

"And she didn't tell you why?" Lydia asked.

"No, she didn't," McKing answered, "She said she didn't want to discuss it over the phone. We are supposed to get together tomorrow and talk about it."

"Sounds like a good idea," Lydia said.

"Is it really?" McKing asked, "Her being scared is a bad thing and I don't think it is a good reason to get back together."

"I think you should listen to what she had to say," Lydia said, "And not make judgements until she is finished. I'm not defending the choices that got her to where she is, however, understand that right now she needs you."

"And you aren't going to tell me anything," McKing said.

"One, she is going to tell you everything tomorrow," Lydia said, "And second, if you have missed the clues up to this point I really can't help you."

"I guess I wait until tomorrow," McKing said.

"Listen to her," Lydia said before ending the call. She put in the numbers McKing and given her before putting the phone back to her ear. It rang several times before it was answered.

"Hello?" it was Justin's voice.

"This is Lydia. I was wondering if you had time on your hands. It is paid."

"Is this a job?" Justin asked.

"Sorta," Lydia answered, "I have been working on a job that is not the usual kind and I need some help with it. But only if you have time; if you don't I'll find someone else."

"I have some time," Justin said, "What does this involve?"

"Do you have time this evening to meet up?" Lydia asked.

"In an hour or so," Justin answered.

"Meet you outside McGregory's Corner," Lydia said.

"Okay," Justin said. Lydia ended the call and put her phone away as Dalton came outside. He sat down on the swing.

"Caitlyn is asleep?" Lydia asked.

"Out without a worry," Dalton answered, "You're sick, aren't you?"

"Who was the man in the park the other day?" Lydia asked, "Caitlyn said you don't like her around when you talk to him."

"He owns the only legitimate security company in town," Dalton said, "I don't think she needs to hear him because he tends to be rough and callous."

"Think he'll give you a job?" Lydia asked.

"He has offered multiple times," Dalton answered.

"Why haven't you taken him up on it?" Lydia asked.

"Because Raymond pays better," Dalton answered, "And I thought I needed the money to support my family."

"And now?" Lydia asked.

"His offer is considerably better than his last one," Dalton answered, "He lost one of his managers and needs to find a replacement in a hurry, but everyone with the necessary qualifications won't leave their positions in other companies. I qualify and he heard I might be looking for another job. He is offering a benefits package that includes the time I need for Caitlyn."

"What did you tell him?" Lydia asked.

"I would come in Monday with my decision," Dalton answered, "I didn't want to appear too eager, but I'm not sure I can turn him down. "

"Probably a good idea to go legitimate," Lydia said.

"Would you go legitimate?" Dalton asked.

"No," Lydia answered, "But you have a daughter to think about and an ex-wife to get rid of."

"How sick are you?" Dalton asked, "Just sick or dying?"

"We are all dying," Lydia said, "Every time we exhale, we are breathing out our live force."

"If I wanted to listen to that type of shit, Megan would still be around," Dalton said.

"Did you call your lawyer?" Lydia asked.

"I did," Dalton answered, "But he off for the weekend, so I left him a message about what you told me and asked for him to call me on Monday. You have somewhere to go tonight?"

"There is an issue I need to sort out," Lydia said.

"Like taking out Raymond?" Dalton asked.

"Not my target," Lydia answered, "I'm aiming for someone who is working as an independent contractor. He is selling to one of the companies Raymond owns."

"But Raymond may be caught up with this person?" Dalton asked.

"That depends on how close his ties are to that particular company," Lydia answered, "He could claim he didn't know what was going on."

"Yeah, he could," Dalton said, "But the police know how much he is involved with his companies. He knows what is going on, whether it is legal or not."

"Do you remember the name of the obstetrician Megan went to when she was pregnant with Caitlyn?" Lydia asked.

"Dr. Hanson," Dalton answered, "He was the only obstetrician in the city at the time. I don't know if that had changed. He was big on women hiring mid-wives if they could afford it and if the women were healthy."

"There an agency the mid-wives belonged to?" Lydia asked.

"No, they worked through his office," Dalton answered, "Because usually they did home visits and only used his examining rooms if there was a specific reason. Why?"

"I'm wondering if Dr. Hanson is still in business," Lydia said.

"Again, why?" Dalton asked, "You are in need of a doctor, but not that kind."

"Because the obstetrician Dr. Chase seems to be getting a lot of business directed his way by the other doctor in town," Lydia answered, "And it seems strange to me."

"I would consider it down right strange," Dalton said, "Dr. Hanson only ever passed patients off to mid-wives when Caitlyn was born."

"I'll have to try calling on Monday," Lydia said.

"This have to do with Raymond?" Dalton asked.

"Highly likely," Lydia said.

"I'm not sure I want to know any more than," Dalton said as he got to his feet. He stopped just before opening the door and turned back to Lydia.

"You haven't smoked you evening cigarette," Dalton said.

"I had one this morning," Lydia said, "And my doctor told me I should limit them."

"And the cravings haven't gotten to you yet?" Dalton asked.

"Probably still high off the oxygen," Lydia answered.

Dalton appeared to be thinking about saying something. He was quiet for a minute.

"Good night," Dalton said before going inside.

"Good night," Lydia said. Once she heard the door lock, Lydia got down off the porch and headed to her car.

When Lydia pulled to the curb near the car, she saw Justin was already waiting for her. He did not immediately notice her car as he was closer to the door of the bar than she could park. However, he did check at the movement. Justin came to the car once he saw it was Lydia in the driver's seat. He got into the passenger seat and closed the door. Once he had his seat belt on, Lydia pulled away from the curb.

"I have to warn you this isn't a high paying job," Lydia said.

"What is this job?" Justin asked.

"I was asked by a woman named Elizabeth to track down her stolen baby," Lydia answered, "She had been dating a guy who claimed he didn't mind she was pregnant with someone else's child. Once the child was born, the man took off with her daughter. She went to the police, but they don't have the resources to keep the search up. I have been trying to track down this man, but he gives a different name to each woman he deals with. I have found three women he has stolen babies from and there is another pregnant who is likely living with."

"We're thieves," Justin said, "Is there something we are supposed to be stealing?"

"Mostly evidence," Lydia said, "There are files under your seat from an adoption agency I broke into to see if I could track the babies."

Justin reached under the seat and pulled the files out. He flipped through them but did not say anything for a few minutes.

"And you need to find more evidence?" Justin asked.

"No," Felicia answered, "I have a line on the man behind the kidnapping and I need to figure out where he lives, where he works, and where he might be hiding more evidence."

"You're talking a stake out," Justin said.

"I did ask if you had time," Lydia said, "And you will get paid for it."

Lydia parked her car between street lamps on a street with mostly apartment buildings and a couple corner stores. There were plenty other cars parked along the street and despite it being late evening there were lots of people out.

"Isn't that Felicia?" Justin asked pointing out three people on the other side of the street. There was a couple and Felicia along with them.

"Yes," Lydia said, "Now keep your eye out for a man who is lurking around and following her. There was a poster with a picture of him in the stack with the files."

"This poster?" Justin held up the poster Natalie had given Lydia.

"That is him," Lydia said.

"I don't see him," Justin said.

"Keep an eye out," Lydia said.

Felicia and her companions went into one of the apartment buildings.

"Does this have something to do with Felicia?" Justin asked.

"Yes," Lydia answered, "He is stalking her."

"Why would he be stalking Felicia?" Justin asked.

"Because she appears to be available and she is pregnant," Lydia said, "And if you tell McKing before she does, your body will never be found."

"Why would she leave McKing if she knows she is pregnant?" Justin asked.

"Never been in a long-term relationship?" Lydia asked, "Or had a fight over your profession? Or not want to tell someone something you should? Or lied in general?"

"But not telling him?" Justin asked, "If I were him, I'd want to know."

"They have scheduled that discussion for tomorrow," Lydia said, "He can be as pissy and upset as he wants to be without your help this evening. We need to find and follow her stalker."

"I think that is him there," Justin pointed. Lydia looked and saw a man standing at the entrance to an alley near the apartment building Felicia had gone into. He matched the picture from the poster.

"Watching this man is your job for the next twenty-four hours," Lydia said, "If you can find out his name that would be helpful too."

"You're not sticking around?" Justin asked.

"I get bored too easily," Lydia answered, "The other thing you should see if you can figure out his connection to Raymond Stewart."

"He is connected to Raymond Stewart?" Justin asked.

"Raymond Stewart owns the adoption agency this man is selling the babies to," Lydia answered, "I'm not sure if there is any other connection, but if you find one I would appreciate to know that too."

"Okay," Justin said as he tucked the files back under the seat.

"Also it might be a good idea if you are not caught," Lydia said, "McKing told me that Kyle Stevenson was already sent after me for the break in at the adoption agency."

"You are deep into this, aren't you?" Justin asked.

"It happens," Lydia shrugged.

"You aren't scared of Kyle Stevenson?" Justin asked.

"I'm still alive so far," Lydia answered.

"I'm fully warned," Justin said, "I shouldn't get caught and I should try not to be connected to you." Justin got out of the car. He moved into the shadows where he could watch the street without being noticed. Lydia drove away.

CHAPTER NINE

Lydia sat on the swing because of the rain, which had been coming down all morning, had made the railing wet. Caitlyn and Dalton were inside watching princess movies. Lydia had come out because she was craving a cigarette, but had not actually taken the package out and was instead just enjoying the rain. He phone rang.

"Hello?"

"You knew this and didn't tell me?" McKing's voice came over the line.

"Depends on what subject you are referring to," Lydia replied.

"I'm going to be a father and you couldn't say anything," McKing said.

"Well, I told Felicia to tell you multiple times," Lydia said, "But I promised not to say anything until she did. Besides, you could have figured it out the same time I did."

"What do you mean?" McKing asked.

"We broke into Dr. Eric Spencer's office together," Lydia said, "On the door, right under his name, is the fact that he is an obstetrician. You found her file in his office. As you said she had a doctor at a different clinic."

"I only paid attention to the name on the door," McKing said, "Because it was your job."

"And the second time you helped me?" Lydia asked.

"I wasn't paying attention at all," McKing answered.

"So, not my fault you didn't know," Lydia said, "What arrangements did you and Felicia make?"

"She is supposed to be gathering her stuff and I will go pick her up," McKing said, "She'll move back into the house. From there we will figure things out."

"Sounds good," Lydia said.

"I'm going to be a father," McKing said.

"You are," Lydia said.

"I was thinking about quitting the insurance company," McKing said, "But I can't now."

"Why not?" Lydia asked.

"Because Felicia is right," McKing answered, "I don't want to raise my child to think being a thief is okay. I want a better life for them."

"I hope you told that to Felicia," Lydia said.

"I will," McKing said, "The shock is wearing off and my mind is starting to work again. I have to go."

"Talk to you later," Lydia said before ending the call.

She barely put it back into her pocket before it rang again.

"Hello?"

"This is Justin. There was slight issue came up while I was following the man."

"What happened?" Lydia asked.

"He grabbed Felicia," Justin answered, "And her put into the back of a van before the van drove away. Someone else was driving the van."

"Did you call the police and report it?" Lydia asked.

"Yes," Justin answered, "I couldn't follow the van and she is in danger. I gave them all the information about the van as well as a description of him. I only had a partial description of the driver to give them. What should I do now?"

"Wait there," Lydia answered, "McKing is on his way to pick up Felicia because they had agreed on that in their discussion earlier. He needs to know what happened and then you are going to meet me at McGregory's Corner. From there we will discuss what to do next. Did the police interview the friend Felicia was staying with?"

"I believe they knocked on doors in the building until they found the friend," Justin said.

"Then it might be better to meet at McKing's house," Lydia said, "The police will search him out and want to talk to him."

"Okay," Justin said.

"I will see you there," Lydia said. After ending the call, Lydia put her phone away and got to her feet. She went into the house for her purse and keys. She stopped in the living room doorway.

"I have to go out," Lydia said.

"Okay," Dalton said.

"But what about our plans?" Caitlyn asked looking away from the movie and toward Lydia.

"I am sorry," Lydia answered, "We will have to do it another day. My friend needs me."

"We'll be okay," Dalton said, "We'll fill the time we other things and those plans can happen some other time."

"If you have to," Caitlyn said.

"Unfortunately, I have to," Lydia said. Caitlyn went back to focusing on the movie and stuck her bottom lip out. Lydia left.

Lydia arrived as McKing was pulling into the driveway. Justin was with him. They all met up on the front step, but no one spoke as McKing unlocked the door. They went into the living room. McKing slumped down in the chair and rested his head in his hands. Lydia sat down in the other chair while Justin took one end of the couch. They waited for McKing. It was quiet for several minutes before McKing raised his head.

"The guy driving the van is one of Raymond's men," McKing said, "I've seen him before and he works for Raymond. We go to Raymond and demand her back."

"Not a good idea," Lydia said.

"We can't leave her with them," McKing said, "They could be hurting her right now."

"They won't hurt her," Lydia said, "The one man wants her child to be born healthy so he can sell it."

"This is the guy who is kidnapping babies?" McKing asked, "She told me someone was stalking her, but she didn't say it was this guy."

"That is why I have been talking with Felicia," Lydia said, "Because when I spoke to her as a favour to you, I mentioned my investigation due to me bringing up the fact that she was pregnant and we had been in the doctor's office. So, when the guy showed up while she was there and then when she went for lunch, she phoned me. I made some suggestions in hopes it would keep her safe, but apparently it didn't work."

"How could they know where she was?" McKing asked, "The must have known she was coming back here. They grabbed her because she would be safe if she got back here. How could they know that?"

"Her cell," Justin said, "Somehow they got the GPS information from her phone."

"Probably while she was in the doctor's office," Lydia said.

"We need to get her back," McKing said.

"We need to see how far the police can get before we start trying to get her back," Lydia said, "Because interfering in a police investigation is going to get us in more trouble we want to attract."

"I don't fucking care about getting into trouble," McKing slammed both fists down on the arms of the chair. He started to get up.

"Sit," Lydia commanded.

The look McKing shot Lydia was meant to tell her where to go, but the one he got back caused him to sit back.

"It would be much better if the police could track her down and get her out," Lydia said, "As if would be best because then the police would get the guy and

Felicia would definitely be safe. Felicia's safety is a priority."

McKing nodded before letting his chin fall to his chest.

"I probably shouldn't be here when the police arrive," Justin said.

"You should," Lydia said, "Because it explains why McKing is here and not sitting on the curb waiting for Felicia to come out of her friend's building."

There was a knock at the door. McKing got to his feet and went to the front door. Someone identified themselves as police.

Before long Lydia and Justin were left to sit by themselves as the police took over certain parts of McKing's house as they prepared for a ransom demand to be called into McKing. As well as continued questioning of McKing as to whether Felicia had any enemies or there was any reason why someone would want to harm her. McKing did them about the fight, but skip the part about Felicia wanting him to quit his career as a thief. He did tell them Felicia was pregnant, however the police did not seem to feel that had anything to do with her kidnapping.

"We should we do?" Justin asked.

"Everything is under control while he has someone to watch over him," Lydia answered, "But I am worried about what he would do if left alone. Because Raymond will kill him if he tries to meet him to ask for Felicia back."

"I can stay here and keep him from doing that," Justin said, "I can't follow someone around who has disappeared."

"Did you find anything while following him?" Lydia asked.

"He went to an apartment building a couple streets over for several hours," Justin said, "1614 Florish Street. I don't know what apartment he went to though. He didn't go anywhere else."

"Okay," Lydia said, "I'll go to the apartment and see what I can find while you stay here and keep an eye on McKing. Call me if there is a problem."

"Be careful," Justin said, "This guy is more dangerous than he seemed."

"I will," Lydia said as she got up. She left the house and went out to her car. The officer outside had to move one of the police cars to let her get her rental car, but once she was able to Lydia headed for the apartment building.

She parked in the alley behind the building. Getting inside was fairly easy as the back door to the building had an easy lock to get through. Lydia went through the lobby area to the manager's office. She knocked on the door. When there was no answer, she knocked again. There was no answer to the second one, so Lydia went to the list of residents. There was a Michael James listed.

Lydia headed up to the apartment number that had been listed. She knocked on the door. There was a minute before she could hear movement from inside. Then the door opened. The girl was maybe sixteen and definitely did not look anything like the man in the poster, but she resembled the woman from the house.

"Justine Winston?" Lydia asked.

"Who are you?" Justine asked.

"Is Michael here?" Lydia asked.

"No," Justine answered, "He has been here since early this morning. He had to catch a flight for a business trip. He won't be home for a few days. Why? Who are you?"

"My name is Lydia and I'm looking for Michael because he kidnapped a friend of mine this morning."

"You have your information wrong," Justine said, "Michael isn't like that. He's a gentleman."

"He has paid for everything you need and everything for you baby," Lydia said, "He's driven you to your doctor's appointments. He expects nothing from you. He doesn't touch you without your permission."

"So?" Justine asked.

"He's all that because he has practice on other pregnant women," Lydia said, "And why do you think none of them are around?"

"Are you trying to scare me?" Justine asked.

"They aren't around because he took their babies and left the women with nothing but a fake name to give to the police," Lydia answered, "You are no different from any of the rest of them. He kidnapped my friend because she didn't fall into his trap of letting him care for her during her pregnancy."

"You can take your lies elsewhere," Justine said as she started to close the door.

"I'm just delivering the warning," Lydia said, "None of the rest were given one. Get out before you regret it."

Justine shut the door. Lydia left the building. She got into her rental car and started the engine. Rather than go back to McKing's place or Dalton's house, Lydia drove to the address of Justine's mother. She parked at the curb and turned off the engine. Before getting out, Lydia wrote the address for Michael James' apartment on a piece of paper and folded it up. Then she got out of the car and went to the door.

Shortly after Lydia had rung the doorbell, the same woman as before answered the door. This time she was without the small child.

"What do you want this time?" the woman asked. Lydia offered her the piece of paper.

"This is where your daughter is," Lydia said, "I tried to warn her, but she has no reason to listen to me."

"And you think she'll listen to me?" the woman asked as she took the paper.

"I don't know," Lydia answered, "But the man kidnapped a friend of mine this morning because she refused to fall for his gentleman persona. The police are looking for him. But whether your daughter gets away from him is between you and her."

Lydia turned and went back to her car. The woman had not bothered to stand there and watch Lydia leave. She had gone inside and closed the door. Lydia headed back to Dalton's house because she was not sure what else she could do.

Matthew Halbert barely looked up from the game at Calder entering the back room. The man with him looked vaguely familiar, but Matt could not place him. Calder took up his usual position of sitting on a grate.

"What brings you around?" Matt asked.

"This is Kyle," Calder answered, "He has a picture of someone he is looking for."

The name reminded Matt where he had heard the name. Kyle had taken out a picture and offered it to Matt. Matt took it and looked down at it through his reading glasses. It was a black and white photo of a person in a black outfit, which covered head and face. At first glance, there was nothing about the person to suggest their identity. Then something made Matt study it closer.

"I thought I recognized her," Calder said, "But I couldn't be sure and all I know is she showed up at my house with one of your men last week."

"I can't give you much more information," Matt said passing the picture back to Kyle, "She showed up here because Sara's brother got a ransom and he didn't want to go to the police."

"What is her name?" Kyle asked.

"I don't know," Matt answered, "She didn't introduce herself. But McKing seemed to know her pretty well."

"McKing?" Kyle asked.

"He's a thief," Matt answered, "Takes mostly soft jobs. Local talent."

"Where would I find him?" Kyle asked.

"Various bars around town," Matt answered, "You can get his number from pretty much any bartender with the right about of money."

"Not that concerned about getting caught?" Kyle asked.

"He doesn't take jobs the police would give a shit about," Matt answered, "He takes soft jobs. The people who need help but can't necessarily pay and the police can't help or won't help."

"That doesn't sound like a very good thief," Kyle said.

"He is good," Matt said, "He just doesn't use his talents well."

"And she works with him?" Kyle asked.

"No," Matt answered, "She said she was visiting. I got the impression McKing was along as a guide."

"Then I guess my next stop is a bar," Kyle said.

"It seems a pity that you are after her," Matt said.

"Perhaps if you had known her sooner, you could have warned her away from messing with Raymond Stewart," Kyle said. He left and Calder followed him.

"Going to send a warning out?" one of the other players asked, "Especially since she was so helpful to you."

"If she is messing with Raymond Stewart, I am sure she knows what she is doing," Matt said. They went back to focusing on the game.

Lydia rolled over when her phone rang. It was a couple hours earlier than she usually got up. She pressed the button on her phone and brought it to her ear.

"Yeah?"

"The police haven't turned up anything," McKing's voice was harsh in Lydia's ear, "They are utterly useless."

"And what do you think you can do about the situation?" Lydia asked.

"I can talk to Raymond," McKing answered.

"And when your body is never found?" Lydia asked, "What do with tell Felicia when we get her back? What do you truly expect to get out of him?"

"Anything is better than sitting on my ass," McKing said.

"You're gonna sit on your ass for at least another hour," Lydia said.

"Why?" McKing asked.

"Because you disturbed my beauty sleep," Lydia answered, "It will take me that long to shower and drive over."

"Fine," McKing said. The line was silent. Lydia sighed as she sat up.

It was slightly over an hour when Lydia knocked on McKing's door. Justin was the one who answered it. He had circles under his eyes and slumped shoulders

"I'm not sure how much longer I could have kept him from going out on his own," Justin said as she closed the door. They headed into the living room, where McKing was sitting and drumming his fingers on the arm of his chair. Lydia sat down in the chair while Justin collapsed on the couch.

"The police have turned up nothing," McKing said, "They don't believe her being pregnant has anything to do with her being snatched. They didn't discount me talking about her having a stalker, but without his name or description, it is useless."

"We have a description of him," Lydia said, "And the current name he is using. We just don't know his real name."

"I didn't have a description to give them," McKing said.

"Justin gave them a description," Lydia said.

"I did," Justin's voice was sleepy and his eyes were closed.

"So, I guess it is just me without a clue," McKing said. Lydia took out a piece of paper from her pocket and smoothed it out before handing it to McKing. McKing stared at it but did not take it from Lydia.

"Who is he?" Lydia asked.

"My supervisor at the insurance company," McKing said, "Christopher Michaels."

"Considering he has been going back and forth between Christopher and Michael, I guess that makes sense," Lydia said as she got to her feet. She tucked the paper away.

"Where are we going?" McKing asked as he scrambled to his feet. Justin was starting to snore.

"The insurance company," Lydia said, "The girl at his apartment said he was away on a business trip." They went into the hallway.

"He isn't high enough up to get those privileges," McKing said.

"Then let's go see if he is at work," Lydia said, "You're supposed to be a work already anyway."

McKing locked the door on their way out. They got into McKing's car and he drove.

McKing parked in his parking spot in the lot under the building. They got out and McKing led the way into the building. There were plenty of floors and the insurance took up three of them. McKing pressed the button for the top of the three.

"You gonna be able to face him without ripping him to pieces?" Lydia asked as the elevator went up.

"I'm not going to do anything that will prevent us from finding Felicia," McKing answered, "That is the best I can do."

"Fair enough," Lydia said.

The doors opened. Most of the floor was made up of cubicles separated from each other with baffles. Most of the desks had a person sitting at a desk. Many of them were on the phone. The rest were going paperwork. Only a few looked up at them, but no stopped them or spoke to them.

McKing led the way to a row of rooms along one side of the floor. There were several board rooms with the middle being an office. McKing went straight to the office, but the door was closed and locked. The man in the closest cubicle looked over the baffle. He frowned at their appearance, which was far to casual for the obvious business dress of the rest of the office.

"Is Michaels in?" McKing asked.

"No," the man answered, "He has today and tomorrow booked off. Greg came around asking if any of us knew where you were."

"I'm having some problem with my girlfriend," McKing said. The man looked at Lydia, she gave him a cold stare ack.

"Up to you," the man shivered and then sat back down.

Lydia moved to the door and took out her skeleton key. She used it to open the door before stepping inside. McKing followed her.

"Might be better if you act as look out," Lydia said, "You belong here and I don't."

"I would argue the point," McKing said, "But I get your meaning." He stayed close to the door.

"If Michaels is the supervisor, who is Greg?" Lydia asked as she moved to the desk.

"He is the person Michaels leaves in charge during his absences," McKing answered, "Greg technically has no authority over anyone except himself, but he reports people to Michaels who will do something."

"Too much office politics," Lydia said as she started going through the papers on the desk.

"Ever worked in an office?" McKing asked.

"Nope," Lydia answered, "But I've seen it done on TV."

"You sit still to watch TV?" McKing asked.

"When the person you want to spend time with is hooked up to an oxygen tank, you don't go out too many nights," Lydia answered. She shuffled through some papers before moving on the desk drawers.

"I suppose that makes sense," McKing said. Lydia rifled through each drawer in turn. She then turned to the filing cabinet.

"Greg incoming," McKing said. Lydia stopped and looked towards the door as a man in a business suit stopped. McKing and the door were blocking most of Lydia from view.

"What are you doing, Neal?" Greg asked.

"What are you doing, Greg?" McKing asked.

"My job," Greg answered, "Whereas you are late, inappropriately dressed, and in Michaels' office where you are not supposed to be."

"Really?" McKing asked.

"Yes," Greg answered, "Who is that?"

"Who is what?" McKing asked.

"The woman going through Michaels' filing cabinet," Greg said.

"Who?" McKing asked.

Greg tried to push his way into the office, but McKing made himself and the door solid barriers to entry. Greg stepped back rather than get violent.

"I'm getting security," Greg said.

"Go ahead," McKing said. Greg went off.

"Are we in the limited window of getting off the elevator as security it getting on?" Lydia asked without stopping her search.

"The fat guy in the lobby isn't going to want to move," McKing said.

"So, plenty of time," Lydia said.

"Yup," McKing said.

They were quiet for several minutes.

"I think I found something," Lydia said. She took out a file and laid it out on the desk. McKing went over to look at it.

"These are papers for properties," McKing said, "This is an insurance company."

"But the names on the papers are not the insurance company," Lydia pointed to the line she was talking about.

"You're right," McKing said, "Where are they?"

"All over the city," Lydia said as she unearthed a pad of paper and a pen. McKing took them from her and started writing down addresses.

"You're not supposed to be in here," the male voice announced from the doorway. Lydia and McKing looked up to see the security person for the building standing there. Greg was not with him.

"Hey, Earl," Lydia said. McKing went back to writing.

"In seriousness, you're really not supposed to be here," Earl said, "He is, but you aren't."

"How's the coin collection going?" Lydia asked.

"Still missing some," Earl answered.

"We're investigating Michaels for kidnapping McKing's girlfriend," Lydia said, "Do you know about his extracurricular activities?"

"I saw him talking to Raymond Stewart once," Earl said, "After that, I kept my nose out of his business."

"Probably a good plan," Lydia said.

"Make sure everything is as you found it," Earl said.

"We will," Lydia said.

Earl left the office and closed the door most of the way, so it was harder to notice there were people inside.

"Is there a thief in the business you don't know?" McKing asked.

"Sure," Lydia answered, "Lots."

McKing finished writing down the addresses and folded up the paper. Lydia closed the files and then put them back.

"Anything else?" McKing asked.

"No," Lydia said.

They left the office and Lydia locked it behind them. They went to the elevator without incident. Even Greg was not around. They went straight down to the parking level. Once they were in McKing's car, he turned on the engine.

"Shall we start with the first one of these?" McKing asked offering Lydia the list.

"Sure," Lydia answered, "But I've only got a few hours and at some point we should go let Justin know what happened to us."

"Fine," McKing said. Lydia gave him the first address as he pulled out of the parking lot.

Each property was industrial, so they could not just drive by and claim to have seen everything. However, the ones they searched did not have many places to hide a human. They only managed to look at half the list before they had to return to McKing's house. Justin was still asleep on the couch. Lydia left McKing to wake him and headed off to pick up Caitlyn.

CHAPTER TEN

Lydia was leaning against the car waiting for Caitlyn to get out of school when Alicia settled herself next to her. Alicia's usual brown hair had been replaced with chin length bottle blonde hair. The rest her features were the same and suggested her relationship with Lydia and Dalton.

"You have been avoiding me," Alicia said.

"And you think showing up in person is going to change that?" Lydia asked.

"It makes it harder," Alicia answered, "I'm sure Dalton will tell me different."

"Since you're here, what do you want?" Lydia asked.

"You are dying," Alicia said.

"In what way do you mean?" Lydia asked.

"Someone hired Kyle Stevenson to deal with you," Alicia answered.

"That hardly seems like a death sentence," Lydia said.

"What other way would I have meant?" Alicia asked, "How bad is it?"

"Pneumoconiosis," Lydia answered.

"You are shitting me," Alicia said. Some mothers who were walking by glared at Alicia. She gave them an apologetic smile.

"Why do you think I've been sending you all the money I earn to be put into the trust?" Lydia asked.

"I haven't been thinking about it," Alicia said, "How long does the doctor say you have?"

"If I quit smoking a few months," Lydia said.

"No wonder you have no fear of Kyle," Alicia said, "His methods are quick and easy compared to what is awaiting you."

The school bell rang. A moment later, the children came rushing out.

"I haven't told Dalton," Lydia said, "But he knows most of it as I had a hypoxemia attack during an afternoon with Caitlyn."

"Scaring your niece is not a good idea when her world is unstable with her mother abandoning her," Alicia said.

"I know," Lydia said, "And I really didn't mean for it to happen."

Caitlyn came out of her door along with her friend Grace.

"She looks more like her father than her mother," Alicia commented.

"If we didn't know for certain that Megan gave birth, I would wonder how Dalton did," Lydia said.

"She is going to very upset when you're gone," Alicia said.

"Fortunately, she had another aunt to spend time with," Lydia said.

"Lydia, you know better," Alicia said, but she stopped when Caitlyn came running over to them and hugged Lydia. Lydia hugged her back.

"Cait, this is your Aunt Alicia," Lydia said.

"Hello," Alicia said.

"Hi," Caitlyn said, "Auntie said I haven't gotten to meet you because your life is very busy and you don't get to visit."

"She is right," Alicia said.

"Then why are you here now?" Caitlyn asked.

"I needed to talk with Lydia and it couldn't be done over the phone," Alicia answered, "And as an added bonus, I get to meet you."

"You must have a really important job," Caitlyn said.

"Some people think so," Alicia replied.

"You answer questions like Auntie Lydia," Caitlyn said.

"We were taught well," Alicia said.

"Can you play soccer?" Caitlyn asked.

"I've been known to kick a ball around occasionally," Alicia answered.

"Good, because Auntie Lydia can't," Caitlyn said.

"No, she can't," Alicia said, "And it is best to let her sit on the sidelines."

"The soccer ball is at home," Lydia said, "If you two are going to play, we have to get there."

Alicia moved from the back door and opened it for Caitlyn while Lydia went around to the driver's side.

Once Caitlyn was in, Alicia got into the passenger side.

They went back to Dalton's house, where Caitlyn and Alicia spent the afternoon in the backyard kicking the soccer ball around.

Lydia waited until they were busy with their game before slipping back inside. She used her cell to phone Dr. Hanson's office.

"This is Dr. Hanson's office," the efficient voice answered, "What can I do for you?"

"Hi, my doctor recommended me to Dr. Hanson. Is there a time this week I could come in for an appointment?" Lydia asked.

"Your doctor is misinformed," the receptionist said, "Dr. Hanson isn't taking on new patients. The only obstetrician taking new patients in town is Dr. Eric Spencer. Do you have a pen and paper?"

"Yes," Lydia said.

"Here is the number for his office," the receptionist then gave the phone number.

"Thank you," Lydia said.

"You are welcome," the receptionist said and then the call was over.

Lydia checked the backyard and saw they were both busy. She took her keys and left by the front door. She drove to the address of Dr. Hanson's office. There was a parking lot attached to the clinic for her to park her car in. She went inside.

There was a main reception area and then the clinic had two areas; to the right was marked as for mid-wives and the left for Dr. Hanson. The reception area had several women in various stages of pregnancy as well as whoever was there to support them. The receptionist behind the desk was talking on the phone. The words were muffled, but it was the same voice Lydia had spoken with on the phone.

Before Lydia could reach the reception desk, a woman from the right side came out and intercepted her.

"Hello, I'm Brenda," the woman offered her hand.

"Lydia." She shook the hand.

"You'll have to pardon me," Brenda said, "But you hardly look like you need an appointment with Dr. Hanson."

"I need an appointment with Dr. Hanson," Lydia said, "But it isn't medical."

"What is your issue?" Brenda asked.

"Referrals from this office to send patients to Dr. Eric Spencer," Lydia said.

Brenda glanced at the receptionist, who was still busy on the phone, before signalling Lydia to follow her down the left hallway. They went passed the first four doors. Brenda knocked and then opened the fifth door, which was Dr. Hanson's office. Dr. Hanson was seated at his desk and writing in a file. Lydia recognized him from the brief time she had seen him when she visited after Caitlyn's birth.

Dr. Hanson looked up at them. Brenda closed the door.

"What is it, Brenda?" Dr. Hanson asked. He sounded tired, but he was only middle-aged.

"This is Lydia," Brenda said, "She wanted to talk to you."

"You seem tired," Lydia commented as she sat in the chair.

"It isn't from overwork," Dr. Hanson said.

"Then you might want to fire your receptionist," Lydia said, "Because according to her, you aren't taking on patients and I should call Dr. Eric Spencer."

"When did you talk to her?" Dr. Hanson asked.

"Just before coming here," Lydia answered.

"Do you have any proof?" Dr. Hanson asked.

"Sure," Lydia said as she took out her phone, "Dial the number for your office." Lydia offered it to him. Dr. Hanson put in the number before handing the phone back. Lydia pressed the button to call before putting it on speaker phone.

"This is Dr. Hanson's office," the receptionist answered, "What can I do for you?"

"Yes, I called a little while ago for an appointment," Lydia said, "You directed me to another doctor, but I talked to my doctor and he said I should see Dr. Hanson. Are you sure he doesn't have time to see me?"

"As I told you when you called last, Dr. Hanson isn't taking new patients," the receptionist said, "Many doctors had not been informed of the matter. Call Dr. Spencer for an appointment."

"Are you sure?" Lydia added a slight pleading note to her voice.

"Dr. Hanson isn't taking on new patients right now," the receptionist's voice was firm, "Dr. Spencer will take good care of you."

"Thank you," Lydia sounded resigned. She ended the call and looked up at Dr. Hanson.

"Thank you, Lydia," Dr. Hanson's voice held the anger in check, "I will deal with this situation from here."

"How did you know there was a problem?" Brenda asked.

"I didn't know there was a specific problem here," Lydia answered, "But I kept hearing from people that they were being referred to Dr. Eric Spencer from here. I was asked to investigate a situation by one of Dr. Spencer's patients when her baby was stolen. When I started looking into it, several of Dr. Spencer's patients had a similar issue, but I couldn't trace it back to the doctor."

"Have you gone to the police?" Dr. Hanson asked.

"Not yet," Lydia answered, "Because I'm still working on gathering evidence, but once I do they will get it."

"So, we should prepare for an influx of patients," Brenda said.

"We have some issues to deal with before we even worry about that," Dr. Hanson said.

"I will go," Lydia said.

"Thank you for coming to us," Dr. Hanson said.

Brenda showed Lydia out. The receptionist paid no attention to them as they went by. Lydia left the clinic and headed back to Dalton's house.

Lydia was in the kitchen when Dalton arrived home.

"My lawyer got back to me," Dalton said as he took off his jacket.

"And?" Lydia asked.

"You were right," Dalton answered, "Megan doesn't care about Caitlyn and only wanted custody for the child support payments. Where is Caitlyn?"

"Out back," Lydia answered.

"Anyway, the lawyer offered her five grand to go away," Dalton moved toward the patio doors. He stopped and looked out. He froze in place and did not finish his thought.

"She took it?" Lydia asked.

"Alicia is in my backyard," Dalton pointed out the window.

"Yeah, so?" Lydia asked, "What happened with Megan?"

"She took the money to go away with the understanding that I was switching jobs and couldn't give her any more money," Dalton said, "And this morning I went and accepted the job offer, so it was true. What is Alicia doing here?"

"She came to talk to me," Lydia answered.

"Why did she feel she had to come here to talk to you?" Dalton asked.

"I quit responding to her messages," Lydia answered, "And she was worried about my health."

"Why?" Dalton asked.

"Because Raymond has Kyle after me," Lydia answered, "And she was concerned."

"Kyle won't kill you," Dalton said.

"You're the first person with confidence in that direction," Lydia said, "When do you start your new job?"

"I started it right after I gathered my belongings and informed Raymond's security chief that I was going," Dalton said, "There were no hard feelings or any deep concerns. He was sorry to see me go but understood my personal situation had changed enough for me to need a different job. He did not appear to connect me to you and whatever issue you are causing for Raymond."

"Good," Lydia said, "I don't want you or Caitlyn mixed up in whatever happens."

"I'm fine with that," Dalton said.

Lydia's phone rang. Dalton opened the patio door and stepped out before closing it behind him. Lydia answered her phone.

"Hello?"

"We found her," Justin said.

"How are they doing?" Lydia asked.

"Felicia is doing fine with the exception of being scared," Justin answered, "And McKing would be going after Michaels with murderous intent, but Felicia refuses to let go of him."

"And Michaels?" Lydia asked.

"Wasn't around," Justin answered, "Police have a warrant out for his arrest, but they are having trouble finding him. I overheard an officer say his apartment was empty."

"His apartment is empty because I told Justine's mom where she was and what was happening," Lydia said, "The police have any other ideas as to where he might go to ground?"

"Not that I heard," Justin said.

"Have they connected him to Raymond Stewart?" Lydia asked.

"It was Raymond's employee who was guarding Felicia," Justin answered, "And the other two pregnant women. The police know who he works for."

"So, what are they going to do about it?" Lydia asked.

"They are looking for Michaels," Justin answered.

"McKing and Felicia going back to his place?" Lydia asked.

"Yes," Justin answered, "What are you going to do?"

"Have supper," Lydia answered, "And then go see McKing because he has the information I need to find Michaels and Raymond."

"Is that a good idea?" Justin asked.

"It is either that or sit around waiting for Kyle to find me," Lydia said, "If you don't want to be part of it, stay away." Lydia ended the call.

CHAPTER ELEVEN

Knocking on the door caused McKing, Felicia, and Justin to freeze. They had been engaged in meaningless small talk seated at the kitchen table.

"Lydia said she was coming here after supper," Justin said.

"I don't think that is Lydia," McKing said, "Go into the bedroom and lock the door."

Felicia gripped his hand tightly.

"I'll handle it," McKing said giving her hand a quick squeeze, "Go."

All three stood up. Justin and Felicia went towards the bedroom, which they could while avoiding the hallway, which was McKing's destination. He went to the door and opened it. McKing did not recognize the man who stood there. The man could have been anyone in his jeans, sports coat, and work boots. The sunglasses were not entirely necessary as the sun was nearing the horizon.

"Can I help you?" McKing asked.

"Are you Neal McKing?" the man asked.

"Yes," McKing answered, "Who are you?"

"We need to talk," the man said, "Invite me in."

McKing felt a piece of ice developing in his gut, but the man was not leaving him any alternatives. He moved aside for the man to enter. The man stepped inside and went into the living room. McKing closed the door and followed him. The man sat down on the couch. McKing sat down in the chair.

"I need some information involving this woman," the man said taking a piece of paper out of his pocket. He unfolded it and passed it to McKing, who looked it over. He recognized Lydia despite the poor quality and not being able to see her face.

"Why should I give you any information?" McKing asked without looking up at the man.

"I suppose I forgot to introduce myself," the man said, "How rude of me. I apologize. My name is Kyle."

McKing unwillingly looked up at the man, who had removed his sunglasses. Cold eyes looked back at him.

"And I've been told you not only know her but have been seen with her recently," Kyle said.

"Her name is Lydia," McKing found himself saying as he offered the paper back to Kyle. Kyle took it and put it away.

"Lydia Sumeton?" Kyle asked.

"Yes," McKing answered. Uncertainty flickered across Kyle's face.

"Thank you for the information," Kyle said as he got to his feet.

"You don't even want to know where to find her?" McKing asked.

"I know where to find her," Kyle said. He left the living room. McKing heard the front door open and then close. It took him a minute after Kyle left before he could get to his feet. He checked and found the Kyle had indeed left. He locked the door before going to the bedroom.

"They are gone," McKing called through the door. The door opened and Felicia stepped out. She wrapped her arms around McKing and he held her to him.

"Who was it?" Justin asked.

"Kyle Stevenson," McKing answered, "Looking for Lydia."

Dalton was helping Caitlyn with her homework when Lydia and Alicia came into the kitchen. He looked up at them.

"You aunts are leaving now," Dalton said, "Go give them hugs and then we'll get back to division."

Caitlyn put down her pencil and looked up at her dad. Something about his tone, made her look toward her aunts with uncertainty.

"Go," Dalton said. Caitlyn got off her chair and went to her aunts. She looked up at them with worried eyes. Lydia got down to give Caitlyn a hug.

"It is going to be all right," Lydia said, "We're going out for a while. You should be in bed asleep before we get back."

"Is Auntie Alicia coming back with you?" Caitlyn asked.

"Of course, she is," Lydia answered as she let go.

"Of course, I am," Alicia said as she got down to give Caitlyn a hug. Lydia stood up.

"It will be all right," Alicia said, "And not just because we say so, but because it really will be all right. Your dad is just worrying over nothing."

"Are you sure?" Caitlyn looked at Alicia and then Lydia. Lydia nodded.

"Of course," Alicia said, "Now back to your homework, so you can be ready for school tomorrow." Alicia directed Caitlyn back towards the table before standing up. Caitlyn went back to the table.

Lydia and Alicia left the house and headed for Lydia's rental car.

"Did Caitlyn get anything from her mother?" Alicia asked as they got into the car.

"The ability to wrap you so tightly around her little finger you don't realize it is happening until too late," Lydia said. Alicia was silent for a moment.

"Damn, she's good," Alicia said.

Lydia started the car and then pulled away from the curb.

At McKing's house, Lydia parked behind Justin's car. She turned off the engine. Alicia made no move to get out.

"You sure about including an undercover cop?" Alicia asked.

"I'm not looking to kill anyone," Lydia answered, "So, yes, it is a good idea."

"Okay," Alicia stressed the word.

"Come on," Lydia said as she opened her door. Alicia got out as well and they both went to the front door. Lydia rang the doorbell twice. A moment later the door opened and McKing was standing there.

"You look like you're expecting me to be a ghost," Lydia said.

"I just had a visit from Kyle Stevenson," McKing said.

"So, he isn't far behind," Lydia said, "That is good."

"That is good?" McKing choked on the words.

"Going to invite us in?" Lydia asked, "Or are we expected to stand out in the open?"

"Come in," McKing stepped back. He closed the door behind them before leading the way to the kitchen. Felicia and Justin were seated at the table. McKing sat down next to Felicia and she tangled her hand in his.

"How are you?" Lydia asked Felicia.

"They didn't hurt me," Felicia answered, "But I'm very sorry I didn't talk to Neal earlier."

"We need to find Michaels," McKing said.

"Michaels needs to be found anyway," Alicia said.

"Who is this?" McKing asked as if he noticed Alicia for the first time.

"My sister, Alicia," Lydia said.

"I thought you said she was missing with a trace," McKing said.

"Turns out things require you to remember where you filed them," Lydia shrugged.

"Why is she along?" McKing asked.

"Because I felt the need for three people," Lydia answered, "And you're not coming."

McKing started to stand and object, but Felicia pulled him back down.

"Please listen to her," Felicia said, "I don't want to lose you, especially right now."

The war played out on McKing's face for several minutes as everyone else waited. It was getting hard to tell which side was winning.

"You owe me a favour," Lydia said, "I'm calling it in right now that you stay here."

McKing sighed.

"What do you need from me then?" McKing asked.

"Raymond's offices," Lydia answered, "You're the local here."

"The office building on Barley," McKing said.

"No wonder Dr. Spencer has an office there," Lydia said, "Cheaper rent."

"Raymond occupies the first floor," McKing said, "The rest he rents out. You think you'll find Michaels there?"

"Michaels has to be somewhere," Lydia said, "And taking shelter with Raymond makes sense. Though the connection between Michaels and Raymond is still a mystery to me."

"Michaels phoned Raymond before he left," Felicia said, "Michaels was rubbing in that Raymond owed him despite everything Raymond had already paid."

"That kind of behaviour can lose you friends," Alicia said, "Maybe Raymond won't mind if we dealt with Michaels."

"First we have to find him," Lydia said, "And we should go."

Justin stood up.

"You want my key?" McKing asked.

"It would help," Lydia answered. McKing got to his feet and Felicia let him go. He went into the other room and came back holding a key card, which he offered to Lydia. She took it and tucked it into a pocket.

"Let me know when he is caught," McKing said as he went back to sitting next to Felicia. Once again she took his hand.

"Of course," Lydia said.

Lydia headed for the front door while Alicia and Justin followed her. They left the house and walked to Lydia's car. Alicia got into the back leaving Justin to get into the passenger seat.

They did not talk as Lydia drove. She parked in the underground parking lot same as the previous times she had been there. There was the same amount of cars parked in the same positions, except for the expensive car usually parked away from the rest. That one was missing.

"I don't think Raymond is here," Lydia said as they headed for the elevator, "His car is missing."

"Probably best," Alicia said.

They went to the elevator door. Lydia used McKing's card key and the door opened. They got in and Lydia pressed the button for the first floor. It was a very short ride before the doors opened again. They stepped out and into a hallway. There were no doors along the inside wall, but there was a couple on the outside wall.

"Raymond's office will be in the centre," Alicia said.

"How do you know?" Justin asked.

"Previous experience," Alicia answered.

"Let's just look for him," Lydia said, "And keep together." She started down the hallway. The other two followed her. They tried both doors, but these led to storage rooms. The end of the hallway turned into another similar hallway. The first door was another storage room.

As Lydia reached for the knob of the second door she stopped. Justin was about to ask when Alicia put her finger to her lips. He listened and could then hear the voices the other two had heard. Both voices were male. Lydia gently turned the knob and pushed slightly. The door opened a crack and she held it in place. There had been no sound to alert the people in the room. The voices were clearer now.

"You're going to be next," the first voice said.

"Why would I be next?" the second asked, "I haven't done anything wrong."

"They will connect me to you and then you'll be out of business," the first voice said.

"Because you met women in my waiting room?" the second voice asked, "That hardly connects us. And they aren't going to catch me with the money from the payments, so all they have is conjecture."

"People have gone away with less," the first voice said.

The doctor, Alicia mouthed. Lydia nodded.

Alicia made an after-you gesture. Lydia pushed the door all the way open. The voices stopped as Lydia stepped into the room followed by Justin and Alicia. It was another storage area, but space had been cleared for a table and some chairs.

"You aren't allowed in here," Michaels said as he got to his feet.

"Of course not," Lydia said, "But we're here now and we aren't leaving without what we came from. Which includes you."

"And you the hell are you?" Michaels asked.

"The person Elizabeth James hired to find her baby," Lydia answered.

"You're the one screwing up this whole operation," Michaels said. His hands became clenched fist.

"I think there are better scams you can run that hurt people a lot less," Lydia said.

"At five thousand a pop, it is hard to beat the one I am running now," Michaels said.

"You need to broaden your horizons," Lydia said, "Five thousand a baby ain't big time."

Michaels moved toward Lydia with both fists swinging. Lydia ducked below his arms and put her full weight into hitting him in the stomach. She moved out of the way as he collapsed forward.

"I suppose the idea of coming quietly is off the table," Lydia said.

Michaels cursed her as he staggered to his feet. Lydia hooked his ankle and caused him to fall to his knees. He winced and tried to get to his feet again. Lydia kicked him in the side of the head and he collapsed to the floor. This time he had been knocked out.

Lydia pulled his arms, so his hands were behind his back. She put a pair of handcuffs on him.

"Now you," Lydia said turning to Dr. Spencer.

"I have nothing to do with him," Dr. Spencer held up his hands as if to prove his innocence, "I was just asked to keep him company."

"We already heard enough to know you are in league with him," Justin said moving to Dr. Spencer. Dr. Spencer did not fight as Justin handcuffed him.

"Let's go," Lydia said. She and Alivia took Michaels between them while Justin and Dr. Spencer led the way. They went back to the elevator and down to the parking lot. Lydia opened the trunk of her car. She and Alivia squeezed Michaels in.

"I guess we have to put this other one in the back seat," Justin said.

"Are you sure there isn't room in here?" Alicia asked.

"I promise not to cause any trouble," Dr. Spencer said.

"Already too late for that," Lydia said as she closed the trunk, "But yes, the trunk is too crowded."

"Then he gets the floor," Alicia said.

"Fine," Lydia said as she went around and opened the back door. Justin put Dr. Spencer face down on the floor. Alicia climbed in without putting her feet down there. Lydia closed the door before going around to the driver's side. She and Justin got in.

Lydia drove them down to an alley near the police station and then parked the car without turning the engine off.

"The files are under the seat," Lydia said. Justin took them out and offered them to her.

"Deliver them along with the other two," Lydia said. Justin gave her a questioning look, but she just opened her door. Both of them got out of the car. Justin retrieved Dr. Spencer from the back while Lydia opened the trunk. Michaels was barely conscious and definitely had not figured out what was happening. With Lydia's help, he managed to get himself out of the trunk.

"You have a limited time with this one," Lydia said, "Because he will run."

"Okay," Justin said.

"And let McKing know when you go to retrieve your car," Lydia said.

"I will," Justin said. Then he directed both men out of the alley.

Lydia got back in the driver's seat. Alicia had climbed through to sit in the passenger seat.

"Well, that is done," Alicia said, "And it isn't too late."

"We'll see what tomorrow brings," Lydia said as she put the car into drive.

Raymond Stewart stared at the monitor showing the security camera footage. His hand curled into a fist and then uncurled. His chief of security stood behind him trying not give into to any of his normal nervous ticks.

"Where is Kyle?" Raymond asked, "This looks like the woman who broke into the adoption agency. Hasn't he identified her yet?"

"I have not seen him this evening," the chief of security answered, "He has also not reported on his progress."

"When he gets in, tell him I want to see him," Raymond said. The chief of security did not move.

"Was there something else?" Raymond asked.

"Yes," the chief of security answered, "You asked for a review of the security from your home the night your wife left."

"And?" Raymond asked.

The chief of security stepped forward to press a button on the monitor. The screen changed to a view of Raymond's front yard. Two figures can be seen running to the corner of the yard, where they go over the fence.

"This is the same woman from the other security footage," Raymond said, "You mean to say this one woman is the cause of all my problems."

"She was the one who helped Bethany escape," the chief of security said, "As well as the burglar at the adoption agency."

"Have you shown this to Stevenson?" Raymond asked.

"No," the chief of security answered, "Because I haven't seen him this evening."

"I think it might be time to call him," Raymond said, "I expect better from my employees."

The phone buzzed. Raymond pressed the button.

"Yes?" Raymond asked.

"Kyle Stevenson is here to see you," his secretary said.

"Send him in," Raymond said. He pressed the button to break the connection. The door opened and Kyle stepped inside.

"We were just discussing your absence," Raymond said.

"I have been tracking down the woman from the picture," Kyle said.

"We have found that she was also the one who helped Bethany leave," Raymond said.

"We already know where Bethany is," Kyle said, "Unless you plan on taking on Kenley."

"I am not as stupid as that," Raymond said, "I've given up on getting Bethany back as much as it galls me to do so. However, I want this woman destroyed."

"You said you have been tracking her down," the chief of security asked.

"Her name is Lydia," Kyle said, "She is a thief and currently visiting the city."

"And I pay you for this?" Raymond's distaste was audible.

"I know how to find her," Kyle said, "But the best way is probably an invitation from you to talk."

"And what am I supposed to be talking to her about?" Raymond asked.

"I'm sure there are plenty of issues for you to iron out with her," Kyle said.

"And why would she come?" Raymond asked.

"Because she wants to trap you so the police can arrest you," Kyle said.

"She sounds less like a thief with everything you say," Raymond said.

"Since arriving in the city, she has been taking on jobs one would not normally associate with her," Kyle said, "But that just makes her easier to lure into your trap."

"You set it up and I'll be there," Raymond said, "But she better be dead by the end of the meeting, or you are never finding work in this city again."

"I know how to do my job," Kyle said. He turned and left the office.

"Right now, you leave me wondering," Raymond said.

Alicia came downstairs to find Dalton sitting at the kitchen table. He was drinking coffee and reading the paper. He did not bother looking up at her as she got her own cup of coffee.

"Don't you have to work today?" Alicia asked.

"Not today," Dalton answered, "Apparently things went better last night than expected."

"We didn't run into Raymond or any of his men," Alicia said, "There was no serious danger. By the way, have you seen Lydia this morning?"

"I haven't seen her since you two left together," Dalton said, "Why?"

"We came in together," Alicia said, "But she isn't in her bed and her rental car is gone."

"Wasn't there when I came back from dropping Caitlyn off at school," Dalton said, "She usually doesn't get up this early and at times doesn't get to bed until after I have delivered Caitlyn to school."

"And you don't think this is strange?" Alicia asked.

"I have spent the last several weeks being told to mind my own business," Dalton answered, "And now you want me to do something else."

"So, she didn't tell you," Alicia said.

"Why would she?" Dalton asked, "Both of you avoid me and avoid giving me any information."

"You were a little early with your getting Caitlyn to say goodbye to Lydia," Alicia said.

"Because Kyle Stevenson is after her, or because she goes through periods where she has trouble breathing?" Dalton asked.

"She is dying of pneumoconiosis," Alicia said.

"I didn't think that was contagious," Dalton said.

"What do you mean?" Alivia asked.

"That is what Robert died of," Dalton answered, "He was her boyfriend for I can't remember how many years. With the way she talked about him, it almost sounded like they might get married and then he got sick."

"It can be triggered by environmental factors," Alivia said, "And her smoking isn't helping matters."

"I believe he smoked too," Dalton said.

They heard the front door open and shortly Lydia stepped into the kitchen.

"Where have you been?" Alicia asked.

"Sitting in a doctor's office sucking down canned oxygen," Lydia answered as she sat down.

"You gonna be okay?" Alicia asked.

"Yeah," Lydia answered, "Because of that, I'm going to be able to breathe easier the rest of the day."

"How long has the doctor given you to live?" Dalton asked.

"It depends on several factors," Lydia answered, "I'm not at the point of sitting around connected to an oxygen tank yet, but if I don't quit smoking my time will be shortened."

"That mean days, months, years?" Alicia asked.

"Months tops," Lydia answered.

"And you were just going to let us find out when you dropped dead?" Dalton asked.

"Better than having you sit around my bedside and watch me waste away," Lydia answered, "My goal is to live long enough to compete in the Houdini Challenge. After that, it doesn't matter."

Both Dalton and Alicia left thoughts unsaid as they sat there. It made the quiet heavy.

"Of course, none of that might matter after this evening," Lydia said.

"Why?" Alicia asked.

"I got a text from Kyle," Lydia answered, "He is arranging a meeting with Raymond for this evening."

"And you are going," Alicia said.

"Might as well," Lydia said, "I hate when I arrange a party and no one shows up."

"You don't expect to kill your guests," Alicia said, "You remember that Kyle is a killer, right?"

"You expect that to scare her?" Dalton asked.

"No, I guess no," Alicia answered, "That is just my gut reaction to facing death."

"You have plenty of years left," Lydia said as she got to her feet.

"Where are you going?" Alicia asked.

"For a nap," Lydia answered, "My sleep got cut off due to breathing problems and I would like to get some more before people starting expecting things from me."

Lydia's phone pinged before she could leave the kitchen.

"Apparently the world is already looking for things," Alicia said.

"It is just McKing," Lydia said checking the message.

"Another crisis?" Dalton asked.

"Yup, an identity crisis," Lydia answered, "When Felicia was trying to get him to go straight, she got him a job at an insurance company. Today he was called into the office. Apparently, one of their supervisors was arrested yesterday and as their employee, he has been asked to the position."

"Another thief off the streets?" Alicia asked.

"He was thinking about staying on with them when he found out Felicia was pregnant anyway," Lydia answered, "He might as well take the promotion to go with it."

"Good for him," Dalton said, "It is probably best for the child not to have parents who are on the edge of spending their life in jail."

"I doubt it would be detrimental to the child's life," Lydia said.

"She tell you that she told Caitlyn she is a thief?" Dalton asked.

"Nope," Alicia said, "Caitlyn told me and then asked what I do for a living."

"What did you tell her?" Dalton asked.

"I own a fighting gym," Alicia answered, "Which meant she had to tell me about you putting back in karate after Megan removed her due to bad energy with the instructor."

"You expected Alicia to lie?" Lydia asked.

"One can never tell with either of you," Dalton answered.

"Later," Lydia said before leaving the kitchen.

Lydia was sitting on a trash can in a half-dark place in the alley. Raymond stopped with plenty of distance, but so they did not have to yell. Both appeared to be alone.

"Kyle said you wanted to talk," Lydia said.

"I wanted to know why you decided to take me on," Raymond said, "You go after my employees, my wife, and my businesses without knowing me or having any reason to be against me. Kyle tells me you are a thief taking on jobs that make no sense for you to take on."

"I came to visit this city for completely unrelated reason," Lydia said, "And a man named Tyler told a friend I was here. I owe Tyler a few favours, so I figured I would listen. You know what I heard?"

"A sob story," Raymond said.

"I heard about a man stealing babies," Lydia said, "As a thief, I see the worst of society and yet I felt that was one worse."

"Those women were specifically selected as ones who would be in a better position in life without the child," Raymond said.

"You may own a lot of things," Lydia said, "But you don't own them or their children. You have no right to make that decision for them. And the betrayal of Michaels didn't help their lives at all."

"I didn't tell him how to do his work," Raymond said.

"No," Lydia said, "But you knew what he was doing and you didn't give a shit as long as he got the results you wanted."

"I have own that adoption agency for years," Raymond said, "The last few years it hasn't made as much money as expected, I needed to do something. People are so big on all those social programs and don't realize certain businesses depend on money from those people."

"As in mothers have more support than before and so less are putting their children up for adoption and it is effecting your bottom line," Lydia said, "It is really pathetic of you and definitely doesn't generate any sympathy from anyone. If the adoption agency isn't making enough money, close it down and find somewhere else to make money. Stealing children makes you lower than bathtub scum."

"That hardly accounts for why you felt the need to take my wife away from me," Raymond said.

"That one wasn't my idea," Lydia said, "That was a request from the women's shelter she had contacted."

"I can't see them paying you enough for such a job," Raymond said.

"I got paid for the job," Lydia said, "And I felt I owed the director for her giving me some information about one of the women who had her child stolen. But your wife was going to get away from you anyway, I just sped up the process."

"You don't know that," Raymond said.

"She had it planned out when I showed up," Lydia said, "I'm not sure why you thought you could abusive to her, Bethany seemed like a fighter to me."

"You know nothing about her," Raymond said.

"Do you?" Lydia asked, "Do you know anything about her? You knew what she looked like, but did you know all her favourite things or how she felt about the world? Because I doubt you knew her that well. If you did, you wouldn't have abused her and she wouldn't have run."

"Your commentary on my life is unnecessary," Raymond said.

"You're the one who arranged this meeting," Lydia shrugged.

"I only came because I wanted something," Raymond smiled.

"And what is that?" Lydia asked.

B. Heather Mantler

"You dead," Raymond answered stepping to one side and out of Kyle's line of fire, "Kill her."

The gunshot echoed against the walls of the alley. It was still going as Lydia fell backward off the garbage can.

"Lydia!" Alicia came out of the dark and ran to where Lydia had fallen. She fell to her knees beside her sister.

Suddenly the alley was filled with police officers. Raymond found himself on his knees and with handcuffs.

"Take him to the squad car," Justin told the officer he handed Raymond off to, "What happened to the shooter?"

"He disappeared," another officer said, "We tried to close in on him, but we can't find him now."

"Keep searching," Justin said. He walked to where Lydia had collapsed. Both Lydia and Alicia were gone. An officer was looking through the trash piled in the alley.

"They're gone," the officer looked at Justin with a shrug. Before Justin could say anything, the captain came over.

"Good job on getting us Raymond and the baby ring," the captain said, "What happened to the thief who was shot?"

"She got away," Justin said, "As did the shooter."

"Keep looking," the captain said, "The thief is probably at one of the clinics in town."

"Yes, Sir," Justin said. The captain went off to be replaced by Justin's partner.

"I'm not sure about your approach to this case," Justin's partner said, "You get put undercover to catch that thief McKing, but he had gone straight and now you can't arrest him. However, you do manage to get the biggest fish in the pond."

"Chance," Justin said, "And some bad luck."

"Better to have your bad luck and most of my good luck," his partner commented before walking away.

Lydia sat on the porch railing and glared at the package of cigarettes she so very much wanted to smoke. Her phone pinged. Lydia put the cigarettes away and took out her phone. She smiled as she read the text.

"Something good happening?" Alicia asked as she sat down on the swing with a mug of coffee in her hand.

"The police found Elizabeth's baby and return the child to her," Lydia answered, "They are going through the files from the adoption agency and trying to get as many babies returned to their families as possible."

"That is good," Alicia said, "But you aren't gonna get paid for the job."

"Somehow, I'm okay with that," Lydia said, "Any feelings of being upset about the matter are being pushed aside by the thoughts that I shouldn't have gone near the whole situation to start with."

"The whole thing does have an unnatural feel to it," Alicia said.

"How is Kyle?" Lydia asked.

"Consider I expected him to succeed at killing you, he is doing fine," Alicia answered, "He has paid all his debts here and is coming home."

"You actually thought he would kill me?" Lydia asked.

"That is what Dalton asked this morning," Alicia said, "I asked him what I was missing and he refused to tell me."

"When you and he got together, I sat down with him and had a talk," Lydia said, "We came to some agreements."

"Like what?" Alicia asked.

"That if he hurt you, he was toast," Lydia answered.

"You threatened to kill an assassin if he did something to me?" Alicia asked, "And he didn't just offer to deal with the threat."

"Well, most of the people around here think I'm dead," Lydia said, "But that is as far as he has gotten there."

"My boyfriend, an assassin, is scared of my sister, who is a mere thief?" Alicia asked, "You are kidding?"

"It was an interesting conversation," Lydia said, "I talked to Dalton about it and I'm headed back to Denise's place tomorrow. You going to stick around?"

"I'm here until Kyle is ready to leave," Alicia answered, "And Caitlyn has me promised to come back from Christmas."

"Some time around family will do you some good," Lydia said, "And if Dalton gets to be too much, tell him off."

"Apparently he is getting used to it," Alicia said.

Lydia smiled. They did not speak as they just enjoyed sitting there.

A Thief in Search of a Baby

ABOUT THE AUTHOR

Heather Mantler is a lover of fairy tales and fables. Her home town is Prince George, British Columbia. Heather is always working on another story as she hopes to finish every story idea that she has ever written down. She was a nominee for the fiction category of the 2012 Prince George Regional Arts and Cultural Awards and short listed for the 2013 John Harris Fiction Awards. Her blog is heathersdomain.wordpress.com. Heather encourages her readers to post reviews on Good Reads and Amazon.

www.ingramcontent.com/pod-product-compliance
Lightning Source LLC
Chambersburg PA
CBHW031316170626
46807CB00001B/435